A Christmas Beginning

The Pemberley Circle Series

Book 1

AP MADDOX

Published by Celestial Light Publishing LLC Utah

PROLOGUE

It is a truth not universally acknowledged, though sufficiently proved by experience, that happiness once secured does not exempt its possessors from the varieties of human nature.

A twelvemonth had not yet elapsed since Mr Fitzwilliam Darcy, of Pemberley in Derbyshire, and Miss Elizabeth Bennet, of Longbourn in Hertfordshire, were united in marriage—an event of January 1813, which, after much trial and misunderstanding, had satisfied the hopes of their friends and silenced the conjectures of their enemies. Their union, founded upon esteem and affection, was daily proving the felicity which attends a just understanding between sense and spirit.

In the first winter of their married life—the Christmas of that same year—Mr and Mrs Darcy resolved to keep the season at Pemberley, and to gather beneath its roof the several branches of their family. Thither came parents, sisters, and friends; and though peace and good-will were the order of the season, they did not arrive unattended by those lesser disturbances which lend animation even to the happiest households.

CHAPTER THE FIRST

"The truest happiness is seldom loud; it resides where affection and good sense are at home."

Pemberley wore its winter as regally as it wore its summer. On the first true snow that held fast upon the Derbyshire hills—no mere flirtation of flakes, but a steady fall upon ground already hardened by frost—the great house prepared to receive its Christmas guests.

From the windows the lake lay pale and still beneath its new covering, its surface sealed to a glassy sheen. Candles stood in orderly ranks, ready to be lighted at dusk; and the air within carried the wholesome scent of beeswax and spice, with the warm fragrance of newly-baked loaves.

Exact in old customs, Mrs Reynolds would allow no holly or ivy until Christmas Eve; the house must look only itself till then. It was Elizabeth's first Christmas as mistress, and though she would have blushed to be accused of triumph, the light in her eyes betrayed the quiet satisfaction of one who had brought her household safely into harbour.

Mrs Reynolds—gratified that her beloved household had found a mistress she could respect—reported that the eastern bed-chambers were fired, and that the cook had perfected a syllabub "which even London would not disdain, ma'am." Elizabeth thanked her warmly, and went on her way—smoothing here a curtain, there the placing of a candlestick.

Darcy found her in the gallery, considering a picture which hung—imperceptibly to others, though not to her—a shade too far to the left. "If the picture inclines," said he, slipping an arm about her waist, "it is because everything in this house inclines to you."

"You have been reading verses, Mr Darcy," Elizabeth returned, smiling. "Pemberley is in danger."

"From poetry?"

"From its master's attempts at it." She stepped back and surveyed the corridor, satisfied at last. "Everything is ready. Mrs Reynolds is a general; I am but a serjeant in her command."

"Then you command even Mrs Reynolds—and that is sovereignty indeed," said he quietly.

Elizabeth—mistress enough to receive homage, wife enough to blush—pressed his hand. At that moment the rumble of wheels announced the first arrivals, and they went down together to the great hall.

The journey from the south had been accomplished in two carriages—the Bennets' and the Bingleys'; for the former, travelling north from Longbourn, had stopped at the latter's new estate in Cheshire, Hollingford Park, to rest a night before proceeding together into Derbyshire. The Bennets' coach was first upon the sweep; and if Pemberley could be improved, it was by the sight of Mr Bennet's ironic brow beneath its lintel, and the prodigious sigh with which Mrs Bennet declared that she had been harassed to death by the cold. Nothing, she vowed, could revive her but a mince-pie, a glass of something warm, and the consoling reflection that three of her daughters were the handsomest married women in England.

The Bingleys followed close upon them, arriving in all good-humour and affectionate bustle. Jane, who had contrived to become even lovelier under the gentle indulgence of happiness, embraced Elizabeth with sisterly affection. Mr Bingley's praises of the roads, the horses, the scenery, the newly-pitched roof of the south stable, and of Pemberley in general, tumbled out so rapidly that even Mrs Reynolds—who had heard every variety of compliment—smiled indulgently in the doorway.

"We have been counting the days," Jane whispered, when the first greetings were over. "There is no sentiment more like Christmas itself than arriving at Pemberley. We mean to behave as if we had never any home but here."

"You shall behave exactly as you please," Elizabeth replied with affectionate warmth.

Caroline Bingley, having come with her brother and Jane, descended from the carriage with the elegance of one persuaded that admiration was her due, and curtsied to Elizabeth with studied grace. Her compliments on the hall were handsomely phrased, though delivered with such deliberation as to seem less the overflow of feeling than the bestowal of favour. She inquired after Georgiana with every appearance of warmth, yet in a tone so carefully measured that it had more the shadow of affection than its substance.

Elizabeth, however, received her with unfeigned kindness. She had resolved that if Miss Bingley chose to practise civility, she could do no less than accept it with cheerfulness. Indeed, there was amusement in the very effort Caroline made; for sincerity never sat so stiffly as when it tried too hard to appear at ease.

Mary, paler than her sisters and much improved by a mantle of sober French grey, was received by Elizabeth with as much kindness as approbation. Kitty, no less noticed, was greeted with a smile and an arch remark that she appeared more blooming than ever.

The third carriage came soon after, having travelled from Newcastle. Lydia darted forward before the footman could assist, running into the hall with her old heedless rapidity. "La! how grand, Mr Darcy! Lizzy— oh, Mrs Darcy, I should say!" She dropped a curtsy with a saucy dip, then twirled so that the fur at her cuffs flew in circles. "And here is Wickham—only the handsomest officer that ever wore a sword! Though you will not have him in regimentals now; he says a married man must not flirt with the maids."

Wickham entered more slowly, bowing with a composure that seemed carefully studied. "Mrs Wickham forgets," said he, with a smile half-pleased, half-apologetic, "that her husband is no longer in service, and must now content himself with quieter honours."

He was civil enough; yet it was plain his place at Pemberley owed more to Lydia's consequence as a sister than to any merit of his own. Darcy's nod to him was grave; and Elizabeth, though she felt the stir of old grievances, had resolved that Lydia should not be deprived of Christmas fellowship. Hospitality was owed, if not indulgence; civility, if not confidence.

Lydia, wholly occupied in displaying the trimming of her gown to Jane and her mother, had no suspicion of the tension her husband's presence occasioned. "Lizzy,

I must know whether your fiddlers will play *The Soldier's Joy*," cried she. "Only do not let Mr Collins read a sermon; I declare I could not bear it."

"Mr Collins is happily far away," said Elizabeth, laughing, "and the musicians promise as many jigs as my sisters can dance."

"Then I shall out-dance them all at the St Stephen's Ball!" Lydia cried, flinging off her pelisse. "Wickham, you shall not sit by the fire like a grandfather; I will have you lively."

"As lively as my wife commands," Wickham replied; and if his cheerfulness were partly assumed, it was, at least, of an improving kind.

Elizabeth, observing, thought if this were but performance, it was, at least, an improved one; and she wished that it might endure long enough to become habit.

On seeing Mary and Kitty, Lydia burst forth with her usual la's and laughter, declaring that Mary looked "quite prodigious fine—only too solemn, as if she were come to deliver a lecture rather than to keep Christmas," and giggling so much at her own wit that Kitty blushed on her behalf; but Lydia, seizing her hands, exclaimed that they must contrive to dance every set together—"for no one hops about with half my vigour, and you shall not be suffered to lag behind."

The sisters' voices rose in cheerful confusion, until Elizabeth, laughing, interposed. "Hush, or none of you will hear the news. Georgiana grows quite impatient for your company, and has contrived a surprise in the music-room. She guards it as jealously as Mr Darcy does the keys of his library. I dare not tell you more, lest she accuse me of treason."

"She is the very kindest of creatures," cried Kitty warmly. "I have long wished to be with her again."

"Her playing has ever been of the truest propriety," said Mary, with measured dignity, "and I am persuaded that any surprise she designs must prove both elegant and improving."

The sisters lost no time in seeking the music-room, where Georgiana awaited them; and before long the sound of laughter, followed by a lively strain upon the keys, reached Elizabeth and Jane, who exchanged a look of unfeigned satisfaction.

When the house had grown tranquil again, Mrs Bennet was at length established near the fire, where she cast a satisfied glance at Darcy, Bingley, and Wickham in turn, pronouncing them the best husbands in all the kingdom. "What other lady can boast such sons? So tall, so handsome, so clever, so attentive—England may keep its dukes and its princes, for I am content with my own gentlemen."

Lydia laughed triumphantly. "And mine is the handsomest of them all! No one dances so well, nor looks half so fine in his regimentals."

"Mr Bennet, for Heaven's sake, say something civil to Mr Darcy," cried his wife.

Mr Bennet, who had already said something civil, and liked Darcy the better each time they met, performed another bow and observed, with calm complacence, "Derbyshire winters are remarkably improved when viewed from Pemberley's fires."

The company's voices mingled in easy commotion; and Elizabeth, observing the circle, looked towards her husband. Darcy returned a nod—so deliberate and solemn it might have been a magistrate's pronouncement. Elizabeth almost laughed at his gravity; yet she understood: with Darcy, such a nod was nothing less than contentment itself.

The music-room, though smaller than the great saloon, was bright with firelight and fragrant with beeswax and polished wood. Georgiana had drawn Mary and Kitty to the pianoforte; and for a little while they indulged in such light talk as young ladies will. Kitty recalled a country-dance where the fiddler broke a string mid-reel; and Mary, more serious, observed that such interruptions might be providential for the sake of modesty. The contrast was so diverting that all three fell into laughter; and Georgiana, to carry the merriment further, struck up a lively tune, which Kitty hummed with enthusiasm, and even Mary joined with a smile.

When the last notes faded, Georgiana turned to them with half-timid eagerness. "I have prepared something for the season—only a little composition of my own—but I would dearly like us to sing it together on Christmas night. Will you indulge me?"

Both sisters assured her they would; and Georgiana laid before them the neat copy she had made.

"It is called *Angel of the Holy Night*," she said softly; "and I hope it will not be thought presumptuous in me to attempt a carol."

She played the opening bars, and Mary, leaning nearer, read the words of the first verse aloud:

Angel of the holy night,
Shining so mild;
Guiding the shepherds' hearts, Seeking the Child.

Peace on the earth below, Mercy's pure light;
All hearts shall worship Him—Love's holy Light.

Her voice faltered into quiet wonder. Kitty, more impetuous, cried, "It is charming! We must learn it at once."

"Indeed, it is beautiful," said Mary earnestly, "and may be sung with real devotion. We shall practise until it is fit to be heard."

The three bent together, voices rising and mingling—uncertain at first, then surer with every line—until the last refrain of *Angel of the Holy Night* was sung so sweetly that they paused, smiling at one another in quiet satisfaction. Georgiana closed the instrument with a gentle touch.

"How lovely it will sound on Christmas night," said Kitty eagerly.

"Indeed it will," Mary replied with approving earnestness, "and with a little more practice we shall do both melody and sentiment justice."

Georgiana smiled, her shyness overcome by contentment. "Then we are agreed—it shall be our offering for the season." They remained awhile longer at the pianoforte, rehearsing a phrase here, adjusting a note there.

In the adjoining parlour the fire burned clear and cheerful, though the daylight had not yet quite withdrawn. Elizabeth poured tea, while Mrs Bennet extolled the perfections of Derbyshire air; and Mr Bennet, seated behind the newspaper, replied only, "So long as it does not rain, I will agree."

Bingley, ever obliging, had stationed himself near the window to observe the road. A few additional guests were expected that evening—gentlemen invited at last in compliance with Mrs Bennet's urgent entreaties that her daughters should not want for partners at the St Stephen's Ball; for her letters had left the Darcys but little peace until they yielded, though it was understood that any attachments which might arise must be the work of inclination alone.

"I daresay they will arrive before dinner," said Bingley, with his accustomed good humour.

"We have every reason to hope so," added Jane, smiling.

Caroline, who had placed herself beside the hearth, observed that Derbyshire hills were picturesque indeed, "though one could scarcely conceive how the wind contrives to find every gap in the landscape."

"The wind is a native, Miss Bingley," said Darcy, his lips curving; "it has the freedom of the county."

Lydia, quite untouched by the chill, had discovered a mirror over the mantel and was adjusting her curls. "If the officers at Meryton could see me now!" cried she gaily.

"They would all wish themselves in Derbyshire, my love," replied Wickham, with an easy composure that surprised Elizabeth by its restraint.

Mrs Bennet, delighted by this gallantry, declared that no company could be pleasanter than their own. "Only let the gentlemen arrive, and we shall make a Christmas to remember."

Caroline, glancing towards the window, observed with languid precision, "Indeed, Mrs Bennet, when the company is so animated, one scarcely feels the want of a ballroom; though I daresay the gentlemen will be gratified to find us already in spirits."

Mrs Bennet, whose curiosity had been mounting all afternoon, leaned forward at once. "And who are these friends, Mr Darcy? You must tell us everything!"

Darcy, with the air of one too well-bred to resist importunity, replied with measured civility, "Mr Hale— a school-friend of mine, and a barrister of Lincoln's Inn. Few men, I believe, unite greater ability with sounder integrity; I count him among the finest of my acquaintance."

Elizabeth, willingly assisting in the introductions, added, "Captain St John comes at Colonel Fitzwilliam's recommendation. He is lately returned to England, and is to spend the winter with his regiment in the north."

Jane, with her accustomed composure, continued the account. "And Mr Hartwell is the curate of Adlington, whose church we attend. We have found him a most sensible and amiable man—his sermons are as well-judged as his conversation."

Mrs Bennet, who had listened with the utmost attention, could not rest without completeness. "And the fourth?" she persisted.

"My friend Ravenshaw," said Bingley, laughing, "a very agreeable man—though I warn you, ma'am, he flatters every lady he meets."

Mrs Bennet clapped her hands. "Four gentlemen! My dear Lizzy, what a charming thought! I declare it will be the happiest Christmas ever known."

Elizabeth smiled, wondering whether her mother's hopes or her husband's patience would be the first to be tried.

CHAPTER THE SECOND

"Where hearts are newly acquainted, civility may disguise what sincerity will afterwards confirm—or withdraw."

Bingley, who had kept his post at the window, turned with cheerful animation. "They are in sight—your carriage has turned into the sweep, Darcy!" His voice carried such pleasure that even Mrs Bennet was satisfied to believe the arrival a triumph of her own contrivance.

Darcy rose, drawing a steadying breath as the sound of wheels echoed in the court. "It seems they are come," he said, half to Elizabeth, who had come near at the sound. "We must give them a warm welcome—though the invitation was urged upon us more earnestly than I could have wished."

Elizabeth's eyes sparkled. "Then we must take care they never suspect it, my dear. They are to be received as warmly as if Pemberley had desired them above all things."

Jane, who had joined them, looked towards the window with her serene smile. "No one could doubt the welcome that awaits them here," she said; "Pemberley wears its happiness plainly."

Darcy smiled, the reluctance yielding to amusement. "Between you both, I am schooled in hospitality better than any sermon could teach. Come—let us greet our guests together."

Four gentlemen were soon announced. The first entered with an air at once composed and engaging; his manner was quiet rather than showy, yet there was in his countenance a warmth which invited confidence. Darcy advanced with real cordiality.

"It is long since I have seen you out of London," said he. "Your chambers must miss their master."

"They will survive the neglect," returned Mr Jonathan Hale, smiling. "For myself, I own no reluctance in exchanging pleadings for snow and society. At Oxford, we younger men always looked up to you, Darcy—your set was already the models of steadiness, and, I daresay, of Latin essays far beyond our reach."

"Then I am fortunate to have escaped before my reputation grew too forbidding," Darcy replied, the corners of his mouth just lifting.

"Oh, it was quite forbidding," said Hale, laughing, "but in the best possible way." His good humour drew a murmur of amusement from those nearest; and in that moment the second gentleman approached.

Mr Elias Hartwell had an air of unstudied propriety which seemed born rather of reflection than reserve. Bingley presented him to Darcy with cordial pride, explaining that his chapel lay scarcely two miles from Hollingford Park, and that he and Jane held him in particular esteem.

Darcy received the introduction with unaffected pleasure. "You are very welcome to Pemberley, Mr Hartwell. My wife will be glad of your acquaintance— she honours good sense wherever she finds it."

"Then I shall hope to deserve her good opinion," said Hartwell, with a modest smile; "though I fear a country clergyman's talk is more humble than entertaining."

"When it is humble," Elizabeth replied pleasantly, "it is generally worth hearing."

Her tone—half playful, yet sincere—won Hartwell's respect at once; and Darcy's glance towards her carried quiet satisfaction. Elizabeth, struck by the gentle intelligence of his manner, thought Georgiana—or perhaps Mary—might find such a spirit most companionable.

Mrs Bennet, however, observed with lively disappointment, "A very worthy employment, sir; yet I hope you will not bury yourself in hymns and sermons. Young ladies, I assure you, prefer cheerfulness to solemnities."

Hartwell coloured slightly, but answered with composure, "Then I must strive, madam, to be cheerful in both."

This reply secured her approbation entirely; she declared she had always admired the clergy—when their livings were good and their sermons short.

The third entrant was Captain Arthur St John, a fine, open-looking man whose sun-browned complexion and ready address bespoke recent service abroad. His bow was frank, his smile unforced, and his bearing that of one accustomed to command without arrogance.

"Derbyshire offers little to remind a soldier of the field, Captain," said Darcy with good humour.

"Then I must be content to find my campaign in its hospitality," returned St John gallantly, his glance including Elizabeth as he spoke. His easy civility drew general smiles, and even Mrs Bennet observed, with great satisfaction, that an officer in a plain coat could be every bit as captivating as one in uniform.

The last to appear was a gentleman of polished address and practised assurance. Though his fortune had been lately made, his manner bore all the confidence of one born to consequence. Bingley stepped forward to present him.

"My friend Mr Felix Ravenshaw," said he with animation. "You must allow me, Darcy, to vouch that he never yet made a gathering less cheerful."

Ravenshaw bowed with practised grace. "Mr Darcy—Mrs Darcy—it is an honour long wished for. Your house is famed even in Sussex; yet I find its welcome exceeds its reputation."

Elizabeth returned the civility with warmth; and when Bingley introduced his sister, the newcomer's attention quickened.

"Miss Bingley," said he, "I begin to believe Mr Bingley's praise of his family was modest after all. Pemberley wears its winter as if to rival its guests."

Caroline, surprised into colour, replied with studied composure, "You are too obliging, sir. The house would shine with far less contrivance."

"Then it must be the company that lends the lustre," he said, his glance lingering just long enough to be particular.

She inclined her head, perfectly pleased to find herself again the object of distinguished notice.

The company now complete, Elizabeth excused herself to fetch her younger sisters who were in the music-room. As she approached, the soft strains of *Angel of the Holy Night* reached her ear; she paused, unwilling to break their harmony. When the last note faded, she entered with a smile.

"My dears, you sing so sweetly I might have forgotten the hour altogether—but the cook would never forgive me if dinner grew cold."

Kitty looked up in protest. "So soon? We had just begun again!"

"There is another reason you must come," Elizabeth said, glancing at Georgiana with a mischievous smile. "New guests have arrived—and wait to be introduced."

"New guests?" cried Kitty, brightening. "Pray, who are they?"

"Friends of Mr Darcy's and of Mr Bingley's," Georgiana replied, colouring slightly. "They join us for the Christmas festivities."

Kitty's eyes sparkled. "Then perhaps we shall have dancing after all!"

Mary closed her music-book with dignity. "If they are sensible men, they will come to enjoy the season, not to make themselves necessary."

Elizabeth laughed. "Then you must forgive them if they try."

She drew Georgiana forward, Kitty fluttering beside them, and the four returned to the parlour, their cheerful voices mingling with the murmur of conversation. Introductions were soon made with all due civility, and the party passed to dinner.

At table, Mrs Bennet lost no time in her usual admonitions. "Now, Kitty, you must not cough so— you were always the greatest cougher," she declared, though Kitty had not made a sound. "And Mary, you must not be correcting the carols when they are attempted, if you value my poor nerves."

Elizabeth interposed softly, "We shall hope your nerves, Mama, will appreciate both music and good manners before the night is over."

Kitty coloured; Mary sighed with patient resignation. Mr Hartwell, perceiving their distress, turned the talk with kindness. "Madam, your daughters need no correction from me—save to say their voices must do honour to any hymn they choose. Indeed, Miss Bennet," he added, addressing Mary, "I should value your opinion on congregational singing; it is a subject close to my heart."

Mary, a little surprised, replied with earnest civility, "Music may be an aid to devotion when rightly chosen, sir—though I fear it is too often made a display."

He observed that *God Rest Ye Merry Gentlemen* should be sung with plainer harmony, to encourage timid voices. "When people are given a part they can perform," he said, "they are proud to perform it. No music is so fine as that which invites the humble to join."

Mary's expression softened. "Those are sentiments most worthy of a shepherd."

He coloured, yet answered quietly, "I endeavour to be."

"That is good," said Mr Bennet dryly. "Real concern for the parishioner—particularly the common sort—is exactly what a good clergyman should possess."

Their talk continued with mutual respect, leaving Kitty to breathe in peace—until Captain St John across the table, caught her curious glance at the faint scar upon his temple.

"Ah! you have discovered my villainy," he laughed.

"This is no wound of battle, but of my own folly. I slipped upon the ice as a boy, and learnt that the Dutch have better balance than I."

Laughter went round the table, and Kitty, half-startled, half-pleased, laughed too. "You have skated in Holland, sir?"

"Indeed; the frozen canals are a world of their own. The Dutch skim along as though born to the ice, while I—" he touched the scar with mock gravity, provoking renewed mirth.

"Are you skilful at the sport?" she asked eagerly.

"Skilful? no," he smiled, "but steady enough when fortune is kind. Have you ever attempted it, Miss Kitty?"

"Never."

"Then we must amend that. I have brought skates; and if the lake is firm to-morrow, it would give me great pleasure to guide you over it."

Kitty's countenance brightened. "Indeed—I should like it above all things."

"Then it is settled," he said; and the promise hung pleasantly between them.

Darcy, overhearing, smiled faintly; and Elizabeth, catching the look, thought there could be no harm in an innocent frolic upon the ice.

Mr Bennet, overhearing only the last exchange, raised a brow half in humour, half in doubt, before turning to Hale, who had engaged him upon field boundaries and the rights of common land.

After dinner, at Elizabeth's request, Georgiana seated herself at the pianoforte in the drawing-room— a larger instrument than the one she used for practice, its tone rich and commanding. The room, warm with firelight and expectation, grew still as she began a Purcell air, her touch steady and clear. Pleasure deepened as she turned to lighter strains suited to the season.

When she asked whether any might assist her, Hale modestly confessed that, though he had not played of late, he could attempt the flute if she desired. Georgiana, with a smile that shewed she did, accepted at once; and he soon proved himself equal to the task. Elizabeth, watching beside Jane, felt her heart warm at the sight; Georgiana's manner, once so timid, now bore the ease of one who both gives and receives pleasure. Darcy's eye, resting on his sister, betrayed the same satisfaction, though his countenance, as ever, was more reserved.

When the piece ended, Georgiana turned to her companion with a blush. "You have quite carried me, Mr Hale; I should never have ventured it alone. I must thank you for lending me both courage and harmony."

He bowed slightly. "The sweetness of your part, Miss Darcy, would have graced any accompaniment. I count myself fortunate to have been admitted to it."

Darcy, drawing near, said quietly, "You have given my sister her ease, Mr Hale; you have my thanks."

"It was already hers, sir," returned Hale; "I had only the pleasure of being present when she found it."

At Kitty's and Lydia's urging, they played again—this time a set of country dances. Lydia instantly seized Wickham's hand and drew him smiling to the floor, declaring she would not have him idle while others made merry. Bingley, ever first to the floor, claimed

Jane; Darcy, not unwilling, followed with Elizabeth. Kitty was led out by Captain St John, whose gallantry lent her an air of consequence; Mary, after gentle persuasion, accepted Hartwell's hand; and Caroline, half-resigned, was surprised by Ravenshaw's easy bow.

"May I hope for one dance, Miss Bingley?" he asked. "If only to prove that elegance is not confined to the graces of this room."

She assented with dignity. "Very well, sir; but I warn you—I dance only as the occasion requires."

"Then let us make the occasion worthy," he said, smiling; and she found herself, despite intention, both flattered and amused.

It had been long since Miss Bingley had danced without calculation, and she was surprised to find the exercise agreeable.

Round and round the sets went, until Georgiana, catching her brother's approving eye, played with a spirit that surprised even herself. Hale's flute wove about her melody with grace, their partnership admired as much as the dancers.

When at last the figures ceased and the company caught breath, Hartwell spoke gently. "Miss Darcy, might we close with a carol? For my part, I think no merriment is better crowned than with a strain of devotion."

Georgiana looked to Elizabeth, who nodded in approval; and she began *While Shepherds Watched Their Flocks by Night.* Mary's eyes brightened—quietly, not demonstratively—and she joined on the second verse, her voice clear; Kitty followed; Hartwell added his tenor, and the harmony filled the room with sweetness.

When the final chord faded, silence lingered before Mrs Bennet burst forth. "Well! Did I not always say our family had more music than any in Hertfordshire? Mr Bennet, you must own it—you must indeed!"

Her husband, glancing up from the chair where he had resumed his paper, replied in his usual tone of irony, "So often have you told me, my dear, that I am astonished anyone in Hertfordshire dares to sing at all."

Laughter rippled through the room, and the spell was gently broken. Elizabeth, looking round, saw Kitty bright with the promise of skating; Mary quietly gratified; Georgiana composed and happy; Caroline not displeased by Ravenshaw's attentions; Lydia content with Wickham at her side; and Darcy meeting her gaze with eyes of tranquil affection.

It was happiness—of the tranquil, domestic kind which neither display nor contrivance could improve; the very happiness, she thought, which Christmas at Pemberley seemed expressly designed to bestow.

CHAPTER THE THIRD

"Good intentions may begin in company, but their proof must lie in solitude."

Morning broke bright and silent, the sky a porcelain blue behind the trees. The frost, which had held the hills for days past, had given the lake a polish like glass— firm and gleaming enough now to tempt even the cautious. The lawns, white as linen, bore tracks where deer had crossed in the darkness.

After breakfast, the household divided, as households will. Mrs Bennet claimed the warmest sofa; Mr Bennet retired, with evident satisfaction, to Darcy's library; while Jane and Elizabeth accompanied Mrs Reynolds to consult upon the arrangements for Christmas Eve.

Captain St John sat in the entrance-hall, skates in hand, waiting with the air of one who hoped to be recollected. At the sound of light footsteps he looked up to see Kitty and Mary descending the great staircase, their cloaks already in place. He advanced at once, addressing the younger Miss Bennet with a smile.

"I am come, Miss Kitty, to redeem my promise of teaching you to skate; and, if Miss Mary Bennet would be so good as to join us, I have skates enough for all."

"I am looking forward to it exceedingly," Kitty returned, her countenance bright with expectation.

"I thank you for the invitation," said Mary, with a small inclination; "yet I had only intended to observe."

Mr Hartwell, who had been seated near the window with a small volume open upon his knee, closed it with quiet decision and rose. "Miss Bennet," he said with respectful earnestness, "since it was not your intention to skate, may I beg the favour of your company to the church to look over the carols? I can easily order a carriage for the purpose, should you be so inclined."

Mary looked at him with a trace of surprise, as if scarcely expecting her quiet remark to be noticed; yet her composure soon returned, and she inclined her head. "I am content to alter my plans—provided my sister can do without me."

Kitty, already tugging on her glove, laughed lightly. "Indeed, I can very well. Captain St John will take better care of me upon the ice than you could from the bank."

Mary's reserve softened into a smile, and she turned again to Hartwell, who looked gratified at her acceptance.

At that moment Georgiana, listening from the stair above, called gently, "Might I accompany you? I should dearly love to watch."

"Just watch?" said St John, with playful gallantry. "Of course—though I shall think it my duty to persuade you further."

Georgiana coloured, but smiled; and, in a few moments, she was cloaked and at their side as they set out together.

The path across the frosted meadows was keen and exhilarating, every branch glittering as if dipped in glass. The little party went forward in excellent spirits—Kitty quick with questions, Georgiana attentive, and Captain St John answering with patient good humour. But when the broad, gleaming expanse of ice came into view, Kitty's step faltered; she regarded the skates as instruments of equal promise and peril.

"Courage, Miss Kitty," said St John cheerfully. "The ice is sound, I promise you. Allow me to fix the straps; the first step is always the most formidable."

She laughed nervously. "I daresay it may prove less forgiving than it looks."

"Less forgiving—perhaps; but never unkind to those with a steady arm to lean upon." He knelt with easy confidence; and when he rose, he offered his hand. "There. You will find the ice more obliging than it appears."

With a quick breath, Kitty let him lead her forward. The first glide made her gasp; but his strength and steadiness bore her up, and within moments she was laughing—astonished by the sensation of flight. St John encouraged her with a mixture of patience and playful daring, teaching her how to balance, how to trust the smooth surface, and at last—when her confidence grew—how to attempt the simplest of figures.

"You are a natural," he declared, when she managed a small turn without stumbling.

Kitty, glowing with pride, shook her head. "No—I am only fortunate in my instructor."

Georgiana, watching from the bank with her hands clasped in her muff, called encouragingly, "Indeed, Kitty, you move as though you had skated all your life! I envy your composure."

St John glanced towards her with a smile. "Then I must make it my next task, Miss Darcy, to persuade you also upon the ice."

Georgiana laughed softly and retreated a step. "Oh, sir—I think I am better suited to applauding from here. Though, if Kitty persists, I shall be lost."

When Kitty faltered and would have fallen, the Captain's steady hand saved her, leaving her with the comfortable notion that he might be safely trusted—while Georgiana, still smiling on the bank, thought her friend the braver for having ventured at all.

Meanwhile Mary accompanied Hartwell in the little carriage towards the parish church, its steeple rising clear against the wintry sky. The ride was brief, but his conversation was steady and considerate, never overpowering hers. He asked after the musical tastes of her family; and when she spoke, with quiet conviction, on the value of congregational song, his attentive manner encouraged her to continue.

"It has ever seemed to me," he said, "that music best instructs when it invites all to share its spirit."

Mary regarded him with interest. "That is a sentiment with which I cannot but agree. Too often sacred music, meant to unite, ends by dividing the gifted from the humble."

His look—earnest, yet without vanity—conveyed his pleasure at her words. "I had hoped you would understand me."

The church was cold but peaceful, its stone walls echoing faintly as they entered. Hartwell paused near the organ and explained his hope of introducing simpler arrangements for the Christmas service, that even the least confident villagers might join.

Together they examined the carol-books, their breath rising in small clouds in the chill air. Mary sang a line here and there to demonstrate a point; and though her voice was modest, it carried with a sweetness that startled even herself. Hartwell joined softly, his tenor blending without dominance; and for a few moments the empty church resounded with harmony that seemed to sanctify so new an acquaintance.

As they closed the book, Mary felt a warmth in her spirit which no fireless nave could bestow. She reflected that, while the attention of a gentleman might gratify vanity, the respect of a good man had power to awaken something both steadier and more enduring.

Back at Pemberley, Hale rode with Bingley and Darcy to examine the estate. His remarks on hedgerows recommended him to Bingley at once; and his respect for tenants recommended him to Darcy almost as quickly.

"The law is too often a bludgeon in the hands of those who need it least," he observed, as they trotted along a fence-line thick with snow-laden hawthorn; "yet I have seen it do good, when a gentleman chooses to wield it for justice rather than for pride."

"I have often thought," he continued, "that the true art of law lies not in argument but in patience. Men imagine it a science of triumphs, when in truth it is a discipline of delays."

Darcy, not given to confessions on horseback, said only, "I am glad you are in the profession, Hale."

"Not half so glad as I am to discover a client I do not yet have admiring me," Hale returned; and Bingley laughed so heartily that his horse tossed its head at him.

Ravenshaw found Miss Bingley free to walk upon the south terrace.

"It is a view to humble London," he declared, offering his arm; "and yet I daresay Miss Bingley could rival even this prospect."

Caroline's smile was small and exact. "I am not so presumptuous as to rival the prospect. I venture only to improve what is willing to be improved."

"Your modesty," he returned smoothly, "is as becoming as your pelisse."

She was not insensible to the compliment. There was in Ravenshaw's manner—its quick intelligence, its insinuating warmth—a power to revive in her that flattering sense of consequence she had thought nearly extinguished. He spoke of town with ease: of music; of the best pastry-cook in Bond Street; of the latest picture at Somerset House. He spoke of houses, and how they bore the stamp of their mistresses. And then—lightly, as if stating what every sensible person must allow—he observed, "In truth, madam, the world is outrageously dependent upon fortune. Taste and talent may adorn a household, but it is wealth that enables them to be seen."

Caroline, whose own fortune was comfortable but not inexhaustible, and whose world had lately refused her the one prize she most desired, listened with composed attention. It was pleasant, after so long an interval, to feel herself once more an object of particular notice; her pride, though wounded, was not insensible to balm. Yet there was a glow in her cheek, when she returned, which both Elizabeth's practised eye and Jane's gentler discernment did not fail to read.

In the warmest room of the house, Mrs Bennet found herself as comfortable as she could desire—

mince-pie, warm cordial, and the happy reflection of her daughters' consequence proving all the remedy her spirits required. "Well! I always said there was no house in England to compare with Pemberley," she declared; "and now I am sure of it. Such good cheer in every corner, and such prospects for my girls—why, it is everything I could wish."

Lydia, perched beside her, rattled on about the coming ball, the trimming of her gown, and a bonnet she had seen in Lambton which, if only Darcy might be persuaded to purchase it for her, would render her indistinguishable from a duchess.

Wickham, seated a little apart with a book in hand that he scarcely pretended to read, bore her volubility with a patience that surprised his observers. At last Lydia, with a toss of her curls, declared, "Marriage has robbed you of all your spirit, Wickham. You were ever the gayest officer in Meryton, and now you sit as dull as any parson."

Wickham looked up—not with the flare of irritation Elizabeth half expected, but with a calm that made Jane glance at Bingley in mild astonishment. "It has not robbed me, my dear," he said evenly. "It has given me other duties. I had rather be dull in your service than lively at your expense."

Elizabeth started slightly at the words; for they bore a gravity she had never heard from him before. Lydia laughed and called him a "solemn creature," but she leaned against his shoulder all the same, more flattered than she knew how to confess.

It was just then that Mr Bennet entered from the library, a volume beneath his arm, in time to catch

Wickham's declaration. Behind him came Darcy, Bingley, and Hale, returned from their ride and shaking the chill from their coats. Mr Bennet paused upon hearing the words, as though doubtful whether they deserved a laugh or a sigh; yet his gaze, resting on his son-in-law, betrayed more curiosity than censure. Wickham met it but briefly, with something near to self-defence, before turning again to his wife with a tenderness that surprised them all. Darcy, lingering near the hearth as he removed his gloves, observed the exchange in silence; and though his countenance betrayed little, Elizabeth perceived that he, too, had marked the change.

When Mrs Bennet and Lydia, in the fulness of their spirits, were drawn into a discussion of lace and new ribbons, Elizabeth found herself a little apart with her father and husband near the hearth. Mr Bennet, balancing his volume in one hand, remarked in a quiet tone, "Well, Lizzy, I own myself astonished. Wickham has discovered a new word—duty. I had begun to think it was not in his vocabulary."

Elizabeth, with a look of mingled amusement and gravity, replied, "If he has learnt it at last, Papa, the lesson has not been without cost. But perhaps it is not too late to profit by it."

Darcy's silence carried more weight than words; he inclined his head slightly—his expression reserved; but Elizabeth, who knew every shade of it, read in his eyes a cautious willingness to hope.

At that instant Wickham, leaving Lydia and approaching with a certain resolution, spoke. His manner bore none of the easy effrontery once so natural to him; instead, his voice was subdued but earnest. "Mr Bennet," he began, "I cannot be in this house, amidst so much undeserved kindness, without speaking what has long pressed upon me. I have wronged your family—grievously, thoughtlessly, shamefully. I will not pretend the past can be undone, nor seek to varnish my offences with excuses; but I would beg your pardon, sir, if you can bring yourself to grant it. Believe me when I say, I mean to be a better husband to Lydia, and, if Heaven allows, a more honourable man than I have ever yet been."

Mr Bennet regarded him steadily over the rim of his spectacles, as though measuring both the sincerity of the words and the man who spoke them. His reply, when it came, was dry yet not unfeeling. "Wickham, I cannot say you have chosen your season ill; Christmas is the proper time for confessions—and for pardons. As for the latter—well, I shall reserve judgement, though not good wishes. If you are indeed determined to improve, you will find no one here gainsay you."

Elizabeth's heart stirred at the gravity of the moment; Darcy's first impulse was disbelief, yet there was in Wickham's tone a humility that could not be wholly disowned. And though Darcy remained silent, he inclined his head with a composure that seemed to seal the tacit truce. Wickham bowed slightly, then returned to Lydia—leaving behind a sense that something, however slight, had shifted: fitting enough for a house already preparing for Christmas.

CHAPTER THE FOURTH

"To appear amiable is a common art; to be so without design is a rare attainment."

The company reassembled after dinner in the drawing-room, where a cheerful fire contended with the winter night, and the glossy frames of the family portraits caught the light. Elizabeth, whose satisfaction in her home had never yet diminished by any familiarity, looked about her guests with a gratification which, if not strictly maternal, was something very like it; for when friends are gathered in peace beneath one's roof, it is difficult not to feel a kind of proprietorship in their happiness. Darcy, standing a little apart near the mantel, had that composed air which in him signified perfect contentment—not the solemn reserve which strangers mistook for pride, but that quiet assurance of a man at ease in his own house, and pleased to see it answer every purpose of comfort.

"I propose," said Bingley, all good-humour and animation, "that we begin with music; for I declare I never play better at cards than when a fine air has prepared my spirits."

"Then you play worst at cards remarkably often," murmured Mr Bennet, who had stationed himself at a small table with a volume open before him, though seldom consulted. "But pray let the instrument determine the cards to follow."

Georgiana did not retreat as she might once have

done. Hale—having taken up the flute—approached her with gentle solicitude. "Miss Darcy," said he, "the evening cannot be perfectly amiable unless it begins with your kindness. If you will allow it, I would venture an accompaniment after your first piece; the fault will then lie with me, and the credit with you."

She smiled—timidly, but with a firmness new to those who loved her best. "If you will play with me after I have found my courage in the first, Mr Hale, I shall be grateful."

Elizabeth's glance met Darcy's; and in that quiet exchange of amusement and pride lay all the approval he required.

Mary, who had hovered near the music-stool with a look in which resolve contended with diffidence, was encouraged by Hartwell's quiet offer: "If you will sing, I shall manage the pages—and, should there be fault, let it rest with me." The steadiness of his tone did more than any flourish could have done.

Georgiana began with a simple air—one of those melodies that, eschewing every ornament, flatter both instrument and ear. The tone was modest and pure; but what surprised Elizabeth was not the playing (which had long been excellent), but Georgiana's manner in the pauses. She did not flee the bench; she looked about with an expression that invited, rather than deflected, the company's pleasure. When Hale joined her on the second piece, the room itself seemed to draw a quieter breath; for the flute, with its clear, unpretending voice, knit itself to Georgiana's part as if both had been acquainted since childhood.

Mary, emboldened, followed with a pastoral air—not

showy, but chosen with taste. Her voice, though not powerful, was steady and true; and Hartwell, having placed himself at the stand, turned the leaves with such attentive care that once, when zeal carried him a page too far, he recovered at her glance. The little mistake, far from discomposing Mary, lent her composure. She finished the last verse with a quiet fervour that left the room unexpectedly hushed.

When the general commendations were offered, Wickham—who had listened with an attention remarkable in one not always commanded by music—advanced a step. His manner was quiet; his voice, for once, without the light raillery which had hitherto been his defence against sincerity. "Miss Darcy," said he, "you do a greater kindness than you know. It is not only that you play well—though you do—it is that you make others wish to be as composed and as ready." He bowed slightly, and retreated before embarrassment could attach itself to either party.

Elizabeth observed him, as she did all her guests—though perhaps with more vigilance where he was concerned. It was not that Wickham had become another man; rather, that the man he had always been was trying, awkwardly, to become better. If the attempt was sometimes ungainly, it was nonetheless honest, and therefore of consequence.

Mrs Bennet, who never admired an occasion that did not allow of praise and arrangement, declared that the music had set her quite in spirits, and that if only Mr Bingley would marry every young lady present to her satisfaction, the evening would be perfect. "And I am sure," she added with significant sweetness to Caroline, "there is nothing so improving to the taste as a gentleman who knows how to admire a lady at the instrument."

Caroline, handsome and elegantly turned out (with a plume that understood its own importance), accepted the compliment with a smile perfectly measured. Near her stood Ravenshaw, whose conversation had that readiness which appears to owe little to effort; he listened with an expression of amusement that was not unkind. "Taste," said he, "is improved by fortune as often as by cultivation. A man who can afford to applaud soon learns how."

"Fortune," returned Caroline, with a lightness that did not altogether disguise the attention of her mind, "is an excellent tutor; but I have sometimes suspected she produces a great many mediocre scholars."

"Then let us resolve at least to be rich mediocrities," said Ravenshaw. "It is more comfortable than being brilliant in penury."

"Comfort, sir, is not always the most comfortable aim." Her eyes flashed for an instant, then fell again to composure. "But I daresay we shall not quarrel about it to-night."

Their banter, though easily borne by the room, contained a kernel not lost upon Elizabeth, who thought she perceived beneath Ravenshaw's lightness a habit of estimating the world which might prove troublesome to a woman who desired to be valued for herself. Yet Caroline, for her part, appeared pleased to be so cleverly understood, even when the understanding was not precisely flattering.

The room, animated by music and mirth, was now in

full voice; and Mr Bennet, perceiving that good spirits were mounting beyond his command, rose to reclaim the company for sense—or nonsense—as the case might be. "I have a book," he said, tapping the volume which had served him admirably as an ornament, "which, if read aloud, would put half of us to sleep and oblige the other half to pretend we are not. The alternative is charades."

"Charades!" cried Bingley, whose taste for whatever promoted laughter was perpetual. "We must have them."

"I warn you all," said St John, raising his voice just enough to be heard, "I am uncommonly bad at guessing; I am excellent only at admiring those who guess well."

"That will do perfectly," Kitty returned with cheerful promptness; "for I am uncommonly good at guessing, and shall be very happy to be admired for it." She gave him such a look as might have justified any quantity of admiration, to the general amusement.

Teams were formed with agreeable confusion. Caroline and Ravenshaw, having begged leave to sit out, kept their post near the hearth, content to record the victories and dispense their measured praise. Mary had intended to sit out as well; yet Elizabeth's gentle insistence, and Hartwell's quiet encouragement, won her into the lists. Hale was drawn with Georgiana and Bingley; while Lydia—who claimed every merriment as her birthright—attached herself to Wickham, and declared that if they did not win, it should only be because everyone else cheated.

The first charade—contrived by Bingley and

Georgiana—was acted with a spirit that surprised Georgiana most of all. She spoke a line—only a line—and that softly; but it was her choice to speak it, and the approval it obtained (Hale's glance was as proud as if she had conquered an empire) did not make her desire concealment again. The word was guessed by Kitty in an instant—"Snowdrop!"—and St John, with elaborate astonishment, professed that he should have known it sooner if only she had not been so clever.

Mary's turn brought a little reading; for she suggested that a short passage might frame the next game and elevate the mind without fatiguing it. Hartwell selected a few lines of Cowper, which Mary delivered with a sobriety that lent grace to the sentiment. There was a hush—respectful, unforced. He turned to her, and in the smallest voice meant only for her ear, said, "Thank you." Mary's colour rose; not from vanity, but from the relief of being received exactly as she hoped to be.

Meanwhile, Lydia, impatient of anything that did not immediately produce laughter, tugged at Wickham's sleeve. "Now, my love, we must astonish them. I shall be the queen of something, and you may be the king, unless there is a better part."

"There is always a better part," he answered, smiling, "but I am satisfied with the one I have." He arranged her shawl more securely about her shoulders—an attention which Elizabeth observed with some astonishment—and contrived a small scene that allowed Lydia to sparkle without impropriety. When their pantomime concluded, he guided her, with a quiet word, away from a jest too broad, and she—miracle of the evening—allowed herself to be guided. Darcy's eye, uninvited but not indifferent, marked the restraint with a degree of surprise approaching relief.

During an interval, still at their post by the hearth, Ravenshaw and Caroline conversed; the room, with its pleasant hum, allowed their talk to be at once private and public.

"You have a talent, Mr Ravenshaw," said Caroline, "for being universally agreeable."

"A cheap gift," he replied, "though it yields profitable returns."

"Profitable in consequence, perhaps," she said, "but not in sincerity."

"My dear Miss Bingley, sincerity is a coin so frequently counterfeited that men cease to examine the stamp. They only inquire—will it pass?"

"And what buys most—sincerity, or the appearance of it?"

He laughed. "I am not philosopher enough to answer."

"I suspect you are too much a philosopher to be at ease with any answer."

His eye rested on the room—on the good furniture, the evidence of old respectability made comfortable by new affection. "There is a security in houses like this," he said more gravely. "It is no small recommendation."

Caroline's chin lifted—almost imperceptibly. "Security is excellent, when it is not the whole of a man's ambition."

"Ambition," said he, recovering his lightness, "should not be so large as to frighten away prudence, nor so small as to beg alms of fortune." He bowed, as if he would not press the matter further; but the bow, neat as a seal, left its impression.

At another table, Mr Bennet was discovered by Wickham, who approached with a circumspection very unlike his former airy courage. "Sir," he said, "your judgement in these games is feared by all parties. Might I ask you to arbitrate a dispute? Mrs Bennet declares that Lydia's queen was unmistakably Cleopatra, while Bingley argues for Dido."

"Both wrong," said Mr Bennet, without looking up. "She was Lydia Wickham, which is the only sovereign she aspires to represent." Yet when he raised his eyes, there was no severity in them; and Wickham—taking the jest as a kindness—smiled in a manner almost boyish.

Darcy had watched this approach with a composure that was the fruit of practice rather than inclination. Elizabeth, crossing to him as if to restore Mr Cowper to the table, touched her husband's arm. "You are very good, sir," she said softly.

"I am very much obliged to the present hour," he returned. "It appears to improve us all."

"Even me?"

"You were beyond improving when I married you," said he, with a gravity that did not conceal his tenderness.

The games resumed and scattered; conversations re-formed in new combinations, as they will in an evening of ease. Hale, finding Georgiana near the window where the frost had penned delicate tracery upon the panes, asked if she would attempt a country-dance at the next opportunity, when the musicians could be had. "I am persuaded," said he, "that shyness is only courage in a thin coat. We must wrap it better."

"I have always thought," she said, with a slight smile, "that courage was something one borrowed from a friend until one had a little of one's own."

"Then I am rich," he answered lightly, "for I mean to lend you a great deal."

Mary and Hartwell, in the neighbourhood of the bookcases, had fallen into a conversation of that rare kind which makes one feel sensible without feeling severe. He asked her opinion of the passage she had chosen—not as a pretext for talking, but from a real desire to know. When she ventured a thought—hesitating lest she presume—he received it with such respect that she ventured another. Thus, without design on either side, they discovered that quiet minds may converse very happily.

Kitty and St John, who had grown merry over their own ineptitude at guessing, were surprised to discover that perfectly wrong answers, offered with grace, produce as much happiness as right ones. "You are determined to be delighted," said Kitty.

"Not at all," he returned. "I am delighted by determination." And he looked at her in a way that made the distinction feel flattering.

As for Lydia, she was so well amused, and so much attended to by her husband, that Elizabeth could scarcely persuade herself she beheld the same lively creature whose carelessness had once been the family's alarm. Wickham did not contradict her; he did not flatter her beyond the line where flattery becomes falsehood; and when she verged upon a tale best kept within more private limits, he diverted her with a laughing whisper and a proposal to fetch her a syllabub. It was not perfection, but it was an attempt, and therefore very near to grace.

Towards the close, when the logs had fallen into that companionable glow which invites both conversation and silence, Darcy addressed his sister with a look that was almost solemn in its satisfaction. "You have given us a very pleasant evening, Georgiana."

She shook her head. "It was the room, and the people in it."

"The room," said Elizabeth, "does very well for itself; but the people were mended by your music."

Ravenshaw, taking his leave of Caroline at the threshold of parting for the night, said, "Miss Bingley, I am persuaded that if the world contained more evenings like this, we should all become better speculators."

"On happiness?" she asked.

"On advantage," he replied—smiling, as if advantage and happiness were twins that merely quarrelled for precedence.

Caroline's answering smile was perfectly turned; yet when she withdrew to her chamber, it lingered oddly in her glass, as though the mirror had caught a thought she had not intended to keep. She could not decide whether Ravenshaw's observations had been precisely as she wished them, but they had certainly been what she understood.

Elizabeth, in the last bustle of candles and courtesies, beheld her father shut his book with a snap of entirely contented laziness. "A tolerable set of young people," he announced. "If they continue in this fashion, I shall have nothing to be wry about, and then where shall my reputation be?"

"In the safest hands imaginable," said Elizabeth, laughing.

The corridors received the company one by one; the house settled itself with those small, satisfied sounds which a well-kept home makes when its inhabitants are at peace. And if, under the comfortable quiet, certain currents were felt—ambition in one breast, new courage in another, a labouring conscience in a third— they disturbed nothing essential. The harmony of the evening had not been a deception; it had been a promise—proof that to be amiable without design is the rarest attainment of all.

CHAPTER THE FIFTH

"Affection, though modest in its beginning, will shew itself when truth and kindness give it leave."

As the house bestirred itself to the savour of fresh-baked rolls and grilled ham the next morning, the post was brought in; and among it lay a letter whose large, decided hand Darcy recognised with pleasure. He broke the seal at the breakfast-table, and, after a glance, smiled across at Elizabeth.

She caught his look at once. "Good news?"

"Familiar news, and welcome: Fitzwilliam is on the road north, and begs leave to make Pemberley his quarters for Christmas."

"Colonel Fitzwilliam?" cried Mrs Bennet, who esteemed every colonel a treasure equal to two parsons and a judge. "La! what a charming addition! I am sure there is nothing so agreeable as a military gentleman at a winter party. Officers always dance the longest sets."

Lydia laughed and declared, "Officers dance the longest sets because their legs are better trained than other men's."

Mr Bennet, behind his coffee-cup, observed, "A colonel's legs, like a bishop's sermons, must be equal to every occasion."

"He writes," Darcy went on, "that he is newly returned from duty, tolerably sound of limb, and tiresomely in need of family society."

"Then he shall not suffer," said Elizabeth, her eyes

bright with that household hospitality which had already turned Pemberley into a cheerful court. "Pray send a man to the turnpike—if the roads hold, he may be here by noon."

Colonel Fitzwilliam was earlier than his hour; the prospect of coming snow had made the postilions anxious, and the colonel impatient. He came in stamping, laughing at the weather as if it were a saucy private in need of correction, and shook Darcy's hand with a warmth that dispelled every draught in the hall. Time and service had given him more gravity, but had not subtracted an ounce of his good humour.

"My dear Mrs Darcy," said he, when she came forward, "I am vastly obliged. Had you not received a vagabond cousin, I must have spent Christmas in a miry inn, quarrelling with a goose."

"We should never have allowed it," she returned, giving him a welcome that was part mistress of Pemberley and part friend. "Come to the fire, and we shall make common cause with you against every goose in Derbyshire."

Turning next to Mrs Bingley, he spoke with equal warmth. "And you, ma'am, are kindness itself to endure another guest in your holiday circle. I trust I may be admitted among your festivities without diminishing them."

Jane, with her usual sweetness of temper, replied, "Pray do not say so, Colonel; Christmas is never the poorer for an additional friend, and you are most heartily welcome."

Georgiana stepped forward with a quiet assurance that surprised him pleasantly. "You are very good to come, cousin."

He bent over her hand and replied with warmth, "I could not have stayed away from Pemberley at Christmas, had the whole regiment barred the road."

St John, with the frank good humour of an old friend, came towards him at once; their smiles met before their hands did, and a few rapid inquiries after mutual acquaintances bespoke the comfort of renewed fellowship.

Introductions were then made to those with whom he had not yet the honour of being acquainted.

"Miss Bingley," said Darcy, "I believe you had the honour of meeting my cousin, Colonel Fitzwilliam, at our wedding. Allow me the pleasure of renewing the acquaintance."

The colonel bowed with easy politeness. "Miss Bingley, the pleasure of meeting again is mine."

Caroline curtsied—composed and elegant, perfectly turned out for the morning. "Colonel Fitzwilliam," said she, with a civility that did not overreach its mark, "Derbyshire is kind to return to us so valuable a relation; I hope you will find Pemberley a restorative after your labours."

"You do me much honour, ma'am," he replied readily. "Pemberley prescribes the best remedies—air, a good table, and the sight of those one esteems. I should be cured in three days, were Darcy to consent to be less exemplary."

"I never knew him exemplary except when observed," returned Caroline, with a small laugh; the colonel only smiled, with a kindness that did not encourage detraction.

In five minutes more he had Mrs Bennet charmed by attention, Mr Bennet amused by wit, and Bingley in fits of laughter at a tale of a colonel who mistook a bishop for a bugler.

Kitty found him as ready to speak of skates as of sabres, when, for a moment, he joined her conversation with St John.

"I have promised Miss Kitty a Dutch figure upon the lake to-morrow, should the weather permit," said St John.

"Then I must at least attend," returned the colonel, "to offer applause—and a hand, should it be required. I am too old for tricks, but not for admiration."

"You are not old at all," cried Lydia, who would have flattered a boot if it laced her the faster. "At least not so old as Mr Collins, and we danced him to tatters once at Meryton."

"That is a distinction I shall carry like a medal," the colonel returned gravely; then, with an ease that made his words seem general, he added, "and if time teaches us anything, it is that youthful follies may yet give way to steadier virtues."

Wickham, catching the turn of phrase, inclined his head almost imperceptibly in acknowledgment—an action so slight it might have been overlooked, had not Elizabeth observed it with quiet surprise.

Lydia giggled into her teacup, delighted only with her own wit.

At the hearth, Ravenshaw—casting a glance towards the new arrival's red coat—bent a little towards Caroline. "Pray be careful, ma'am," said he, in a tone of raillery; "Derbyshire is full of good sense, yet even the wisest counties have been known to surrender to a red coat."

Caroline's fan stirred, scarcely more than a breath. "My heart, sir, has never been taken by a colour."

"Then I am reassured," he returned lightly; "for colours fade—but other recommendations, I am told, are more lasting."

If the house that morning possessed a bright complacency, the afternoon disturbed it with a rustle of importance: a second carriage at the gates, the liveries alarming in their certainty, and a card sent up with the uncompromising announcement that Lady Catherine de Bourgh and Miss de Bourgh desired to know if their presence would be agreeable at Pemberley for the Christmas season—having judged that family was always best assembled at holy tides, and that the road from Rosings, though long, was instructive to servants if not to horses.

Elizabeth and Darcy looked at one another in a silence full of comedy. "We are, it seems," said Elizabeth at last, "to be agreeable."

Colonel Fitzwilliam, who had caught the purport of the card, laughed in the best humour. "So I am not the only person whose thoughts run towards Pemberley at Christmas," cried he; "Rosings steers the same course—and at a soldier's pace."

"Then you must be our quartermaster of civility, Colonel," said Elizabeth; "we will furnish the tea, and you the armistice."

"And if the armistice should fail," added Darcy, with a gravity that did not conceal his amusement, "Mrs Reynolds has orders enough in cake to subdue a regiment."

With everyone at their posts, Darcy sent down the message that Pemberley was always at Lady Catherine's service.

Lady Catherine entered as monarchs enter—by right and with inspection. Her eye, travelling over the hall, condescended approval upon the order of the place, rebuked a draught that did not exist, and found Mrs Reynolds satisfactory only because Mrs Reynolds had the good sense never to be otherwise.

"Mr Darcy," she began, before she had removed a single glove, "you have been extremely remiss in not writing to me of your cousin's arrival. I should have been spared the surprise—though I am, of course, equal to it."

"I am delighted to be surprising, Aunt," said Colonel Fitzwilliam, stepping forward with a bow that contained as much mirth as respect would allow.

"Colonel," she returned, with the faintest inclination, "I presume you are not wounded in any essential limb."

"Only the tongue, ma'am, which in my profession is indispensable."

"I had not observed it indispensable in yours," she said, and passed on to bestow a colder greeting upon Elizabeth, whose composure never failed under artillery.

Anne, pale as ever but less pinched, came in her mother's wake like a pale moon in an over-bright sky. Georgiana went to her at once. "I am so glad you are here, Anne," she said softly. "We shall sit by the fire and choose music; and if you are equal to it, we will twine a little garland of holly for my sitting-room."

"I should like it of all things," Anne answered, colouring with that delicate pleasure which attends permission where there had formerly been command.

When the remainder of the party were presented, her ladyship's eye rested, with more than common approbation, upon Caroline. The young lady's handsome style and decided manners appeared to recall to Lady Catherine something of her own earlier consequence; and she was pleased to pronounce that "a young woman who knows how to enter a room has the better part of her education already," adding, with a complacency not wholly unobserved, that Miss Bingley "puts me in mind—at a proper distance—of myself when I was younger." Caroline received the tribute with a curtsy of becoming humility, which did not, however, disguise her satisfaction.

When Ravenshaw was presented, her ladyship's eye sharpened. She catechised him upon his fortune at some length; he owned, with easy propriety, that his capital was chiefly in shipping—now in the hands of partners—together with a small estate near Chichester in Sussex. He answered the rest with becoming ease, and with a zeal for compliment which her ladyship received as no more than was due.

"Shipping," said her ladyship, "is tolerable when converted into acres."

"It is precisely my design, ma'am," returned Ravenshaw. "The best part of my profits is laid by for Sussex; I am already in treaty for a small farm adjoining—contiguous land being, as your ladyship knows, the only land that grows."

"Provided it is fenced, drained, and not scattered like

a beggar's wits," Lady Catherine rejoined. "Partners, too, require governance."

"Mine are men of probity," said he, "and the counting-house keeps to my hours."

Satisfied to this extent, her ladyship concluded by pronouncing him "tolerably well situated." Ravenshaw bowed, visibly relieved, though he bore his triumph with credit.

Caroline listened with very pretty attention; the substance satisfied her, and his steadiness under so much fire did not lessen his consequence.

Colonel Fitzwilliam, passing Darcy with a half-smile, said quietly, "Engagement concluded—our man has stood the shot."

"With colours flying," Darcy returned, his look conveying equal amusement and relief.

The house, being full of happy commotion, allowed two young ladies to slip away unobserved. Georgiana led Anne into the music-room, where a single candle upon the pianoforte made a very quiet cheerfulness.

"I have something to shew you," said she, opening a neat folio. "It is a little carol of my own—*Angel of the Holy Night*. Will you hear it, and tell me frankly if it may be sung at Christmas?"

She played the air without flourish, and, in a voice perfectly modest, sang the first verse.

Anne listened very earnestly, her hands folded as if to keep herself still. "It is—very sweet," she said at last; and then, with more feeling, "It is better than sweet; it is devout."

"Then you like it," cried Georgiana, pleased. "I am to stand with Mary and Kitty; and if you would join us—only where you choose—it would make me very happy."

Anne coloured, and hesitated. "I have never sung before company."

"We will not call it company," returned Georgiana, smiling. "You shall be between Mary and me; Kitty has courage for us all, and I shall keep the time. You need not sing every line. There is a place in the second verse that seems written for you—*'Glory to God on high, / Grace shining bright;*—only that, if you like, and then the last *'Love's holy Light.'*"

Anne's eyes went down to the page, then up again. "Love's holy Light," she repeated softly, as if trying the words upon her breath. "I think—I could venture that much."

"We shall try it together," said Georgiana; and she set the chords very quietly. Anne's voice, though timid, came true upon the notes; it did not thrust itself forward, but went along with the air as if it had always been meant to accompany it.

When they ended, Georgiana closed the folio with a look of contentment not far from gratitude. "You will stand with us?"

"If I may be allowed only that little part," said Anne, still blushing, "I should like it of all things."

"Only that, and no more than you please," Georgiana assured her. "We shall persuade Mr Hartwell to take the pianoforte, and Mr Hale to take up the flute. We shall practise each day until Christmas night, and we shall be perfectly safe."

Anne smiled—a small smile, but entirely her own. "Then I am persuaded too."

They returned by the quiet passage, with a sense—
very gentle, but very certain—that, when Christmas
night came, the carol would have one voice more than
it had in the morning.

CHAPTER THE SIXTH

"A single generous action may weigh more with the heart than years of silent pride."

Dinner had been ordered half an hour earlier to satisfy Lady Catherine's notions of seasonable management. When the door was opened, and the butler announced that dinner was served, Darcy offered his arm to his aunt; Colonel Fitzwilliam attended Mrs Darcy. Mr and Mrs Bennet, Mr and Mrs Bingley, and Mr and Mrs Wickham went in; after them Mr Ravenshaw had the felicity of conducting Miss Bingley. The unmarried ladies followed with the remaining gentlemen in easy precedence.

As Ravenshaw and Caroline went, he lowered his voice for her alone. "I am convinced, ma'am, that Pemberley is never seen to advantage unless one has you to shew it to advantage."

"You give us too much consequence, sir," returned Caroline, allowing herself a small, composed smile; "the house recommends itself."

When they were placed, Darcy sat at the head with Lady Catherine on his right; Elizabeth presided at the foot. Fitzwilliam, seated between Elizabeth and Jane, contrived that everybody should be at ease without appearing to contrive it.

Ravenshaw took the place assigned him at Caroline's side, and, for the first minutes, was scrupulously hers—inquiring whether she meant to be in town for the winter assemblies, and adding, with a glance well directed, that the best-ordered house is that which leaves a gentleman nothing to do but admire his neighbour. Caroline's expression—perfectly finished— acknowledged the attention.

Presently he addressed Lady Catherine above him. "Your ladyship found the Lambton road tolerable?"

"Barely tolerable," answered she. "Postilions ignorant, and a mile of new gravel laid as if fashion could replace sound workmanship."

"I entirely agree," said Ravenshaw. "Method, not novelty, makes a road—and a parish."

"Just so. Method is the soul of order," Lady Catherine pronounced.

"I shall remember your ladyship's rule," said Ravenshaw, with a composed inclination of the head.

Looking across, he turned with measured deference to Miss de Bourgh. "May I hope the journey did not fatigue you?—and is it the south walk at Rosings that lies most out of the wind, or the east shrubbery? I have heard both commended."

Anne paused, as if uncertain she had been truly addressed, and glanced—almost involuntarily— towards her mother. "The—south walk, I believe— when the mornings are still," she said at length, colouring a little.

"Because it is well contrived," interposed Lady Catherine, "and because I insist upon proper intervals for exercise."

"Then Rosings sets the pattern," said Ravenshaw. "I shall be guided by it when I am at home."

Conversation then flowed easily about the table, until

the talk turned to plans for the morrow. Captain St John half rose from his chair and, with cheerful humility, addressed the table. "If the company will pardon my boldness, anyone who has a mind for the lake to-morrow—whether to skate or only to observe—shall find me at their service."

Kitty's eyes shone outright; Georgiana smiled and looked towards Anne. "If we go to observe together," she said softly, "we shall be brave enough to do a very little more."

"Set me on the bank," said Hale, "and I'll do my duty—applaud bravely, and keep the cloaks from running away." Georgiana glanced towards him and smiled a little.

"For my part," said Hartwell, with modest earnestness, "I must go into Lambton to hear the parish choir practise for the Christmas service." He turned a little towards Mary. "Miss Bennet—if it would not inconvenience you—might I beg your company? You shall make of me a critic fit to be corrected." Mary, surprised into colour, answered in a low voice that nothing could suit her better.

After dinner, Lady Catherine signified her pleasure to have whist. "Mr Darcy, you play with tolerable steadiness. Colonel, you will attend me. Mr Hale may complete the table—his profession ought to teach attention."

Mrs Bennet and Lydia, enchanted at the prospect of cards, were instantly in motion. They prevailed upon Wickham to take a place beside them, while Mary was pressed into service at their table. Lydia dealt with exuberant haste, her mother exclaiming over every turn of the cards, and Wickham good-humouredly losing more than he won. Mary, though less animated, seemed quietly entertained by their mirth, observing that "cards, like life, are seldom won by prudence alone." The reflection, though little heeded, was received with laughter, and even Wickham smiled as he played on.

Mr Bennet, who liked nothing so well as seeing a card-table idle, placed himself near enough to observe without being drafted.

Ravenshaw, thus at liberty, found Caroline perfectly at leisure for conversation. He began—very properly—with her brother's good spirits, and proceeded to London, where he spoke of a new singer at the Opera, said to rival last season's favourite; of the endless repairs in Bond Street that inconvenience every carriage; and of the superior civility of tradesmen who know one's direction. Caroline, gratified by so just an attention to subjects she could admire, met him with equal discernment. She did not play with coquetry; she played with judgement, and found that Ravenshaw returned every stroke with agreeable accuracy.

Lady Catherine's table had now attracted every attention. Between the rubbers, when she called Ravenshaw to her side, Fitzwilliam left the whist-table with a smile that belonged equally to his aunt and to amusement. He addressed Caroline with frank civility. Caroline, who valued ease when it was not careless, entered at once into a conversation that suited her well; its tone was lively without presumption, and respectful without design. The Colonel's laugh had the rare merit of being at nobody's expense. Lady Catherine, though her eye seldom wandered far from her cards, appeared satisfied that her nephew's attention was properly bestowed.

Ravenshaw, glancing now and then towards the easy progress of their conversation, betrayed a slight alteration of manner. His attention, which had been well bestowed upon Caroline, now turned to Lady Catherine and Anne, who was seated near her mother. He listened with visible zeal to a maxim upon parish officers, and, when her ladyship said something particularly clever, laughed with such heartiness as to draw the notice of the whole room. He then spoke, with proper deference, of Anne's delicate health, expressing a hope that the mildness of the season might continue to favour her improvement, and that her ladyship's influence would long preserve so good an example of order and charity. Lady Catherine, much gratified, allowed that both were desirable; and Ravenshaw, encouraged by her condescension, withdrew with every appearance of satisfaction.

At whist, Lady Catherine played with an authority that might have terrified any card not printed; Darcy, patient under correction, was rewarded by one approving nod which would have furnished a smaller mind for a fortnight. Hale, who had never yet lost a cause through good temper, contrived to be useful without being brilliant.

In the milder circle, Bingley begged Elizabeth to keep his reckoning, and was grateful when she forgot it as often as himself; Jane and Hartwell laughed at his good humour.

Kitty and St John were discovered at a round of cassino—she intent on victory, he too gallant to dispute it.

"You make no effort to win," said she.

"On the contrary," returned he, "I make every effort to learn." She coloured, and promised to be severe to-morrow—upon the ice.

Wickham, invited to a higher stake, excused himself with an easy civility that did him more honour than acceptance would have done. He crossed the room to fetch Lydia's shawl unbidden; and—observing Anne, who sat conversing with Georgiana, shrink from a small draught—placed a screen between her and the door with such unaffected readiness, that Georgiana thanked him before recollecting that she had never addressed him first in her life.

Elizabeth, catching the action, looked instinctively towards her husband; and Darcy, who was already observing the same scene, met her eyes in silent astonishment. Neither spoke; but both seemed equally at a loss to comprehend what they had witnessed. He then returned to Lydia and laid the shawl gently about her shoulders.

"Oh, Wickham!" cried she, loud enough for half the room to hear, "you are the best gentleman that ever lived!"

"Nay," said he, colouring a little, "the title would sit ill on me. I only do as I ought."

"As you ought?" she laughed. "Then all other husbands should take lessons of you!"

"Heaven forbid," he returned lightly, "that I should be made an example of."

"Indeed, my dear Lydia, you are quite right," exclaimed Mrs Bennet, delighted. "No gentleman could behave more properly! I have always said Mr Wickham had the truest manners of any man in the regiment."

Mr Bennet looked up, his expression half amused, half astonished. "I begin to think that miracles are not confined to Scripture."

When Lady Catherine had won a sufficient number of tricks to establish precedence, she pronounced the evening tolerable and rose. "To-morrow I shall hear the carols, inspect the lists for coal, and determine whether the poor be as well off as they pretend. Colonel, you will attend me." She bestowed a general benediction in the form of advice.

At the door, Fitzwilliam took leave with a smile for everybody. He told St John that he meant to join them on the ice after attending to his morning duties with her ladyship, and begged they would not delay on his account—he should find his way there when released. Then, turning to Caroline, he said, "Miss Bingley, may I hope you will venture to the lake with us to-morrow?"

She was for a moment at a loss, but recovering herself, said with a small laugh, "I am not much used to that sort of exercise, but I believe I should like it." The avowal was modestly spoken; yet her composure did not quite conceal the satisfaction with which it was received.

Ravenshaw, observing the Colonel's parting civility to Caroline—and the pleasure with which it was received—was struck with a degree of astonishment not easily concealed. A moment's reflection, however, restored him to prudence; and turning with renewed zeal to Lady Catherine and her daughter, he paid her ladyship a compliment on the duty of Christmas charity, begged leave to wait on her in the morning for her sentiments on parish order, and concluded with a hope that Miss de Bourgh would not be over-fatigued by so much good accomplished in so short a time. Mortified vanity very soon resolved itself into discretion; and where a young lady's portion was understood to be considerable, his zeal could, with very little effort, become particular.

"You may attend," said Lady Catherine, "if you are punctual." He promised punctuality as if the virtue had been newly invented.

Hale renewed his promise of attending the skating— "as the holder of cloaks, if not the ornament of the ice." Kitty declared that a good audience was half the performance; and Georgiana, smiling, said that she and Anne meant to take that office upon themselves, and would admire from the banks. St John thanked them with cheerful gallantry, adding that the pleasure of such society would make the morning even more delightful.

Hartwell reminded Mary of their engagement for the morrow in Lambton; and she received the recollection with a seriousness that could not conceal its happiness.

At length the party broke up for the night; and, as the room began to empty, Wickham—lingering a little behind his wife and Mrs Bennet, who were recounting to every hearer the agreeable manner in which they had spent the evening—approached Darcy. "Mr Darcy, may I beg a few words with your sister—Miss Darcy?"

Darcy regarded him for a moment, and then, with a composure not wholly unmixed with surprise, called to his sister in a tone of calm command. "Mr Wickham has something to say to you, Georgiana."

Wickham, with a gravity new to his manner, began: "Of all the follies of my youth, none weighs upon me so heavily as my behaviour towards yourself. I trifled with innocence, presumed upon former kindness, and wounded where I ought only to have protected. It is my earnest wish that you should believe me sensible of the wrong, and that you would permit me to assure you of my unalterable regret. I scarcely dare to hope for forgiveness; yet if, in future, I may be thought of not as an enemy, but as one striving to be an altered man, I shall count it the first blessing of my reformation."

Georgiana heard him with evident emotion; her colour rose and fell as he spoke, and for a moment she seemed unable to reply. At length she said, with a sweetness that had more of earnestness than timidity, "Mr Wickham, the recollection of former days has long ceased to give me pain. I hope, sincerely, that yours may cease to reproach you. If you are resolved to act rightly, there is no one who would more rejoice in it than myself."

Wickham bowed low. "You are all goodness, Miss Darcy," said he; and, after a moment's silence, withdrew.

The others having retired, only Darcy and Elizabeth, with Bingley and Jane, remained by the fire. They had been near enough to hear the greater part of what passed between Wickham and Georgiana, and now sat for a few moments in thoughtful silence. Darcy stood musing; Elizabeth, watching him, was silent also; and it was Bingley who first spoke.

"Upon my word," cried he, "if this house continues to work such miracles, I shall have no peace till I bring every reprobate I know to Pemberley!"

Elizabeth laughed a little. "Let us be thankful the season has produced repentance, not reprobation. Yet I confess I am astonished; I had not thought Mr Wickham capable of such humility."

"Nor I," said Darcy gravely. "But repentance, when it is real, must begin somewhere. Whether his will endure is another question."

Jane, ever anxious to believe the best, said gently, "He spoke with such feeling. I cannot but hope it is genuine. Lydia was so happy this evening—perhaps her husband's better conduct may make her so always."

"If so," said Elizabeth, "we must own that Pemberley's Christmas has been better employed than ever we dared hope."

"I am sure Mama is happy," returned Jane, with her gentle smile. "Kitty and Mary seem each to have found companions entirely to their taste."

"A much less mischievous arrangement than I had foreseen," said Darcy, almost smiling.

Elizabeth looked up at him with that expression of mingled playfulness and affection which was all her own. "Then you will be obliged to confess," said she, "that your guests have done you credit."

"I do confess it," he replied; "and if they depart as peaceably as they sit to-night, I shall call it the happiest Christmas Pemberley has yet known."

With this comfortable assurance they parted for the night; and, as the house, once noisy with voices and laughter, grew still, there remained only the falling embers in the grate and the soft whisper of snow against the panes.

CHAPTER THE SEVENTH

"The joy of a household is seldom of one kind; harmony consists in many hearts moving together."

Morning dawned bright and windless, the fields lying silver-white under a hard frost. Pemberley was early astir: servants moved lightly through the passages, fires were rekindled, and the cheerful bustle of breakfast began before the sun had cleared the eastern hills.

Lady Catherine, exact to her word, was already prepared for her expedition to Lambton, where she meant to hear the carols rehearsed and to pronounce judgement on the state of parish charity. She had been heard, even before the tea-urn appeared, giving directions about the hour of departure and the proper order of her calls. Ravenshaw, whose attendance she had graciously sanctioned the night before, hovered in evident satisfaction at having secured so distinguished a conveyance.

Caroline Bingley, entering soon after, found him already stationed near the hearth, cup in hand and spirits in high feather. He greeted her with the polished ease of a man who mistook civility for conquest.

"Miss Bingley," said he, advancing a step, "it seems that fortune has again favoured me with the earliest pleasure of your company. I am to attend Lady Catherine this morning, though I shall envy those who remain here to bask in yours."

She smiled faintly. "You will find little basking in

such weather, sir. The morning is fit only for industry—and thick gloves."

"Then I shall be industrious in my admiration," he returned, lowering his voice just enough to suggest meaning. "A privilege I fear the rest of the company will begrudge me."

"Indeed, Mr Ravenshaw," said she, turning towards the sideboard, "if admiration be labour, you are the most diligent of men."

He laughed—half flattered, half piqued—and was on the point of replying, when the door opened to admit Colonel Fitzwilliam, the colour high in his face from a brisk ride, and his manner as buoyant as the air without; his entrance, as usual, seemed to bring the morning in with him.

"I believe, Miss Bingley," said he, "you are one of those ladies who make the choosing of breakfast a principle. I admire such steadiness; the rest of us are mere amateurs, content to take what Providence and the cook provide."

Caroline turned towards him with a smile both polite and amused. "You do us injustice, Colonel. There is no art in it—only self-preservation. A wrong choice at breakfast may ruin the temper for the whole day."

"Then the household is safe," said he, selecting a slice of ham. "Your example will keep us all in good humour."

She coloured slightly, but her smile remained. "A charitable hope, Colonel. I shall try not to fail so important a charge."

"I have no fear of it," he returned, his tone easy and good-humoured.

It was a light exchange; but there was an ease in it that surprised even Caroline. Fitzwilliam's manner combined frankness with a shade of respect that asked nothing in return; she felt neither the need to impress, nor to defend herself.

At that moment Lady Catherine's voice, distinct and unhurried, was heard from the far end of the table.

"Fitzwilliam," cried she, "you must persuade Miss Bingley to accompany us. I shall be in want of female companionship. Miss Bingley will do the office perfectly."

He turned at once, bowing slightly. "My dear aunt, I am honoured by such a commission." Then, with a smile to Caroline, he added, "Miss Bingley, I am ordered to make you useful—will you forgive the tyranny?"

"With pleasure," she replied. "I can imagine no better use for a morning so fine."

Lady Catherine nodded her satisfaction. "Excellent! We set out within the hour. I detest delay almost as much as I detest ice. Mr Ravenshaw, pray see that the steps are cleared. I will not have my neck endangered for want of diligence."

"You may rely upon me, madam," said Ravenshaw, moving off at once, his bow correct though his haste imperfect. His expression, however, betrayed a moment's irritation as the Colonel, still standing near, offered Caroline his hand to assist her to her seat.

"I am glad, Miss Bingley," observed Lady Catherine, noticing none of it, "that you are so obliging. A sensible companion is a rarity."

"You do me honour, ma'am," Caroline returned, her

composure unshaken, though her eyes betrayed amusement at the bustle her acceptance had produced. Fitzwilliam smiled and took his place at the table, while Lady Catherine settled back with the air of one who believed she had arranged the world to her satisfaction.

Her gaze, still ranging the company, soon alighted upon Mr Hartwell, who had been speaking quietly with Mary. "And you, sir," said she, "are you also bound for Lambton? I trust you will not overcrowd my carriage."

"Indeed no, madam," he replied with respectful ease. "Miss Bennet and I purpose to go in a small carriage to hear the carols rehearsed, and to offer a few humble suggestions to the curate respecting the congregational singing—how it might be made simple enough for every voice to join."

"A most becoming employment," said Lady Catherine, satisfied to have regulated even their intentions. "You may follow us at a suitable distance."

Her pronouncement delivered, she reached for her tea, and all returned to their breakfasts, the cheerful hum of conversation soon restored.

Mr Bennet, who had entered in time to hear this decree, could not resist a smile; and Elizabeth, catching his eye, perceived that Mary's zeal promised rather more pleasure than piety. Hartwell, however, seemed perfectly content with the arrangement; and his look of attentive gravity suggested that devotion might, in this case, extend as much to his companion as to the music.

Darcy and Elizabeth attended their departure at the great door, the morning air bright and still above the frosted park. Lady Catherine's voice, issuing from within the carriage, was already heard in counsel to the coachman; the Colonel stood beside his horse with patient good humour; and Caroline, stepping in after a graceful exchange with him, appeared perfectly composed. Mary's countenance, meanwhile, expressed a solemn pleasure quite her own, while Hartwell's civility wanted nothing but time to become tenderness. Elizabeth could not observe them without a smile; and even Darcy owned that the morning promised to be lively.

The small cavalcade set forth: Lady Catherine's carriage first, drawn with stately deliberation through the iron gates; behind it, Fitzwilliam on horseback, attending as escort; then Hartwell and Mary followed at a distance proper, yet near enough to be thought of the same company.

Ravenshaw, having contrived to secure a place opposite Lady Catherine and beside Caroline, felt that fortune at last had remembered him. The Colonel rode without, and within the carriage all was warmth, civility, and rank. It was not lost upon him that no scene could better display his consequence.

He began, as duty required, with a few well-turned compliments to Lady Catherine on the judicious order of her servants and the excellence of the equipage; but he spoke them with a moderation that allowed his attention to wander, as if by accident, towards Caroline. When her ladyship discoursed on parish duty and the virtues of the poor, he listened gravely; then appealed to Caroline for confirmation that female influence was the surest guard of domestic virtue. Her reply, composed yet animated, so pleased Lady Catherine that she immediately called upon her for further opinion on the improvement of cottages. Caroline's answer—"that gratitude was most lasting when joined with comfort"—won instant approval. Ravenshaw, eager to shew himself of similar mind, added a few observations so judiciously expressed, that her ladyship was pleased to adopt them as her own before proceeding to another subject.

Pleased with the course of the discussion, Ravenshaw contrived to prolong it—inquiring, as if by courtesy, whether Caroline had often seen such orderly villages elsewhere, or whether she thought the discipline of Lambton church might profit by her ladyship's example. His manner had all the warmth of gallantry restrained by decorum; and if Caroline perceived his design, she betrayed it only by a composed civility that was no less provoking for being perfect.

At length they arrived at the little stone church of Lambton, its windows gleaming with frost-flowers, and found the singers already gathered for rehearsal. The interior was bright with winter light; the air smelt faintly of fir and candle-smoke. Lady Catherine took possession of the foremost pew and arranged her gloves for listening. Colonel Fitzwilliam, having attended her to her seat, placed himself beside her at the aisle end. Miss Bingley followed and seated herself directly behind them, her countenance composed and attentive. Mr Ravenshaw took the outer end of the same pew, his air of deference disguising a design to be at once near Lady Catherine and within sight of her companion.

Hartwell and Mary, who had entered quietly from the side aisle, were soon busied in examining the hymn-books and exchanging observations with the curate.

Mary's face bore its usual air of seriousness, but her manner was mild and composed; she spoke of the advantage of simplicity in sacred music—how the humblest voices might join with better effect when the harmony was less adorned. Hartwell, listening with a look of real admiration, added a few remarks so justly expressed that even the curate seemed grateful for suggestions so politely given.

When the choir began practising their hymns for the season, Caroline listened with attention not wholly given to the tune. Fitzwilliam, turning slightly, observed that he had never before heard such power from so small a company. "They sing as if heaven might hear them," he said quietly.

"I hope it does," she answered; and for a moment her usual composure softened into something like emotion. "It is strange," she added, after a pause, "how happiness can make one humble."

He looked at her with surprise. "You are happy, then?"

"I think I am," said she simply. "And you?"

"I have every reason to be—this morning among them."

Their eyes met for an instant—just long enough to attract the notice of Ravenshaw, whose own attention had lately strayed from Lady Catherine's observations on the proper management of the choir. The gentle intelligence passing between the pair stirred in him a sensation half envy, half irritation. His countenance instantly recovered its polished calm as he leaned forward, eager once more to appear absorbed in her ladyship's remarks on the subject.

"You are perfectly right, madam," he declared, "nothing so elevates the spirit of devotion as a well-regulated choir. Discipline in music, as in morals, must begin with those qualified to command. Your ladyship's guidance will assuredly bring every voice into its proper harmony."

Lady Catherine inclined graciously. "I have always said so. The best intentions are useless without direction. They must be taught their parts—and to keep to them."

"Indeed they must," cried he, and though his eyes wandered now and then towards Caroline, it was only to renew his professions with greater fervour.

Caroline, unaware of Ravenshaw's divided attentions, continued her quiet exchange with the Colonel in cheerful composure. Her observations were sensible and well expressed, showing a mind attentive rather than showy. Fitzwilliam, who had expected reserve, was agreeably surprised by the ease with which she conversed, and by the calm discernment that marked her manner. There was nothing forward in their discourse, yet something in its simplicity gave it a particular grace. Ravenshaw, observing their quiet understanding, felt his triumph of the morning lose some of its savour; the warmth of the carriage no longer appeared so agreeable.

When the rehearsal concluded, Lady Catherine rose first. Colonel Fitzwilliam immediately stepped forward to offer his arm, which she accepted as her due. Ravenshaw, who had stationed himself near the pew door in hopes of distinction, hastened to open it for her passage; the service, though humble, carried all the appearance of zeal. Having conducted his aunt a few paces down the aisle, Fitzwilliam turned back and, with quiet propriety, presented his arm to Miss Bingley. She accepted it with composed grace, and together they followed Lady Catherine towards the porch, while Ravenshaw's deferential smile concealed the mortification of one who had been forestalled at every turn.

The sun lay bright upon the snow outside, and the air rang with the jingling of harness. Colonel Fitzwilliam attended his aunt down the steps and handed her into the carriage before turning back to Miss Bingley, who waited at the porch. With a quiet word of courtesy, he offered her his hand to descend.

"I hope," said he, "the morning has not been too cold for you."

"On the contrary," she replied, "I have seldom found so much warmth in December."

"Then I am rewarded," said Fitzwilliam with a smile. He conducted her to the carriage, where Lady Catherine was already seated, and handed her in. Mr Ravenshaw followed.

Her ladyship signalled to her coachman, and the equipage set forward through the glittering snow towards the overseer's cottage, that she might satisfy herself respecting the state of the parish poor and the just distribution of coal. Ravenshaw, restored to his seat opposite her, renewed his homage with redoubled energy—discoursing upon duty, charity, and the blessings of rank— while his thoughts strayed, against his better judgement, to a lady whose smile was at that moment directed elsewhere.

The carriage returned to Pemberley a little after midday. The hall, bright with firelight, filled with the agreeable bustle of their return. Her ladyship, pleased with her own morning's exertions, permitted Elizabeth and Fitzwilliam to attend her to the drawing-room, where she seated herself with an air of satisfied consequence to rest before luncheon.

While Lady Catherine and her party had gone into Lambton, Captain St John and his companions turned towards the lake, where the frost—bright, companionable, and secure beneath a veil of snow—promised both amusement and a little display of courage.

The air was keen and clear; a pale sun hung over the hills, and every sound—the ring of steel, the rustle of cloaks, the small shrieks of laughter—seemed sharpened into cheerfulness.

"Now, Miss Kitty," said St John, fastening her strap with mock-solemnity, "you have not forgotten your lessons, I trust. Grace before speed; elegance before enterprise."

"I remember every word," she declared, laughing. "Though the ice may not."

"Then we shall remind it," he replied. "Lean forward—yes, exactly so!—and now, let us shew the county what perseverance can accomplish."

Her first circle was one of perfect composure, the second of daring ease; by the third, she was laughing outright as St John matched her pace, their turns tracing bright patterns upon the glassy surface.

Mr Hale, who had undertaken the charge of the cloaks and now presided over them like a magistrate of fashion, applauded heartily. "A triumph of instruction, Captain! Your student is the most elegant of skaters!"

"Do you hear that, Georgiana?" cried Kitty, half-breathless. "He says I am elegant."

"I should say so," answered Georgiana, smiling. "You have more confidence than I could summon in a month."

"Confidence is only a well-fed goose in disguise," said St John, wheeling round them with easy mastery. "Once you catch it, it will follow everywhere."

Anne, wrapped in a fur-lined mantle, stood beside Georgiana on the bank, watching with quiet enjoyment. "I think," she said softly, "that to watch is the safer pleasure."

"Then you shall be my audience," said Georgiana, laughing. "I will risk one turn myself; but if I fall, you must promise not to look severe."

"You shall not fall," said Anne gently, and smiled as Georgiana stooped to fasten her skates.

Hale came forward at once, drawing on his own pair. "If Miss Darcy will accept a companion," said he, "I should be honoured to prove that steadiness can sometimes be shared."

"I shall be grateful for it," she replied, the colour rising slightly in her cheek. "But I warn you, I make no progress without encouragement."

"Then we are already equal," returned he; "for I have never skated with such incentive."

He offered his hand, and together they moved cautiously on to the ice, his voice low and cheerful as he guided her round a turn. When they came again to the bank, she was laughing outright. "I have survived—

73

and I begin to think courage may be catching."

"Then I must keep near you," said he, smiling.

Anne, watching them with quiet pleasure, observed that friendship was the surest support on slippery ground; and Hale agreed that he had never found a safer proof of it.

Lydia, unwilling to be outdone in any merriment, had persuaded Wickham to escort her on to the lake as well, declaring that she meant to learn in a single morning whatever others took a week to master. Her first attempt very nearly fulfilled the prophecy in reverse; but Wickham, steadying her with patience, bore her laughter and her tumbles with good humour.

"If you will cease to giggle for one moment," he said, "you might find your feet."

"Then I should lose all my courage," cried she, "for my courage lives in my laughter!"

"So long as it keeps you upright, I am satisfied," he replied; and they set off again, to the amusement of every spectator.

Thus the lake, under a bright and windless sky, became a scene of happy confusion—gliding figures, tumbling ones, and an unceasing exchange of mockery and applause.

When at length the luncheon bell sounded from the house across the park, summoning the skaters to return, St John declared it the finest morning of the season; and Kitty—still laughing—answered that he had only to teach her waltzing on ice next time.

As the company quitted the ice, the air had softened; a thin mist hung above the lake, turning every breath to silver. Cloaks were gathered, hands were offered, and laughter carried lightly across the frozen meadow. St John lingered to ensure no glove or muff had been left behind; Kitty insisted upon one last turn, and contrived to fall into his arm with such neatness that no one could decide whether it was art or accident.

Georgiana, a little flushed from her short venture, declared the morning perfect. "It is a pity," said she, "that all happiness must end in hunger."

"Not so," returned Hale; "for hunger is the best proof of happiness achieved."

"Then you are the happiest philosopher I know," said Anne, smiling.

CHAPTER THE EIGHTH

"Gratitude improves the taste of every pleasure."

In the west anteroom, Caroline, having removed her gloves, lingered a moment to warm her hands. She had scarcely approached the fire when Ravenshaw entered, his expression composed, his tone that of a man assured of his reception.

"Miss Bingley," said Ravenshaw, advancing with that air of easy possession which had first commended him to her notice, "Fortune is kind indeed; she has delivered you from the perpetual crowd. I feared that cousin of Darcy's—Colonel Fitzwilliam, is it?—would never leave your side long enough for any other to claim a moment's conversation."

Caroline's composure did not falter. "Colonel Fitzwilliam has been civil to many this day, sir; I cannot think myself particularly distinguished."

He smiled with practised indulgence. "Ah, but you are. He lingers where he finds attraction, though one must pity him—a soldier with little fortune and less prospect. Gallant in his way, but hardly a companion a woman of discernment would choose for life. Surely you see the disparity?"

Her colour rose. "I see only a gentleman who conducts himself with honour."

"Honour, yes," he allowed. "But honour is a poor substitute for consequence. Tell me honestly—has he pressed his suit? Offered you anything beyond trifles?"

Her eyes flashed. "No, Mr Ravenshaw. He has made me no such offer; nor have I reason to expect it."

He leaned nearer, his voice low. "Then permit me to speak plainly. If you were to withdraw your favour from that quarter—prove that such an attachment holds no place in your heart—I might be disposed to make an offer of a very different kind. You and I, Miss Bingley, might command a circle far above what a modest colonel could ever compass."

The suggestion, though wrapped in courtesy, struck with all the force of presumption. Caroline drew herself up.

"You presume too much, sir. Colonel Fitzwilliam's friendship is mine to value; and no inducement could make me renounce it. As for any offer from yourself, pray spare me the condescension of speaking further."

For the first time Ravenshaw faltered; the smoothness of his smile wavered. "I meant only—"

"I believe you have said enough," she interrupted, curtseying briefly before quitting the room.

Upstairs, she paused only when the door of her chamber closed behind her. The winter light lay cold upon the mirror as she seated herself before it, regarding the face she knew too well.

She had long prided herself on discernment—on reading a gentleman's consequence at a glance. Yet she had nearly been blinded, not by admiration, but by vanity: by the flattery of attentions too artful and too convenient.

Ravenshaw's words still echoed—his sly disparagement of Fitzwilliam, his hints of conditional favour, his presumption that she might barter friendship for ambition. The insult was intolerable.

Her thoughts turned, with shame, to her former designs: the contrivances by which she had sought to part Jane from her brother; the eagerness with which she had once imagined Georgiana might secure her advancement; the petty attempts by which she endeavoured to lessen Elizabeth's consequence in Darcy's eyes. In all this she perceived, with mortification, that she had been guilty of the very ambition which Ravenshaw had now betrayed. The reflection stung her pride; yet in its sting was relief—for every scheme had been defeated to her own advantage. Jane was happy, Elizabeth honoured, Georgiana serene.

She rose, straightened her shoulders, and said softly—as though her reflection might bear witness— "I will not be courted as though I were a prize to be haggled for. Better the honest regard of a poor colonel than the empty professions of a man who cannot speak without calculating."

Her dignity, so shaken, began to recover; but it was not pride alone that steadied her. A sense of justice, long neglected, pressed upon her conscience. Whatever follies she had once committed, she would henceforth be a truer friend to those she had wronged—to Jane, to Elizabeth, to Georgiana—and even to Colonel Fitzwilliam, whose sincerity had proved more valuable than any glittering pretension.

When she descended again, her composure was perfect; yet something gentler, almost luminous, softened her manner. Her eyes, once restless in search of advantage, rested now with quiet steadiness upon those around her.

Jane, adjusting the ribbons of her gown before the fire, looked up as Caroline approached. "My dear Jane," said she, with unaffected warmth, "that colour becomes you perfectly; I do not think I have ever seen you look more elegant."

Jane, surprised yet pleased, thanked her with a gentle smile; and Caroline, turning then to Elizabeth, added, with equal sincerity, "Your house is everything a home ought to be—graceful, cheerful, and full of kindness. I begin to think that nothing recommends refinement so truly as contentment."

Elizabeth, who could not mistake the tone, returned her a look of real regard. Neither she nor Jane spoke of the alteration; yet their exchanged glance acknowledged it was felt.

After a short pause, Caroline turned to her brother with quiet seriousness. "Charles," said she, "you have always possessed an ease with people which I once mistook for mere good nature. I begin to see it arises from something better—a wish to make others happy as readily as yourself. It is, I think, the truest form of grace."

Bingley coloured slightly, protesting that if he had any such merit, he had learned it by example; but Jane only smiled and said that his lessons had been long practised.

A few minutes later the party was assembled for luncheon, though Hartwell and Mary had not yet returned; it was supposed they had lingered in Lambton. A little way behind the others, their progress had been checked by a small crowd gathered before one of the cottages. A man lay upon the frozen ground, his tools scattered beside him

"It is old John Turner!" cried one of the women in alarm. "He slipped from the roof, and his leg—oh, his leg is broke for certain!"

Without hesitation, Hartwell sprang from the carriage. "Miss Bennet, will you come? We must see how best to move him." He was at the man's side in a moment, kneeling in the snow. "Courage, Turner—you are safe now. Can you hear me?"

The man, his face white with pain, gasped that he had been mending the thatch when the ladder gave way. His leg lay at an angle that made Mary's breath catch; yet, steadying herself, she knelt beside him and took his hand. At that moment she perceived his wife and children standing a little way off—the woman weeping into her apron while the youngest clung to her skirts.

"Do not be afraid," said Mary gently. "Your husband is in good hands now. Mr Hartwell and I shall see him safe to Pemberley, where he will be properly cared for."

Hartwell gave her a glance of approving gravity. "If you will keep him calm, Miss Bennet, I will see to the rest. We must lift him without jarring the limb. You there—men—lend your strength a moment."

The men stepped forward at once, and under Hartwell's direction they raised the injured man with steady care and bore him to the carriage. Mary followed, soothing him with quiet assurance. The cottagers, much relieved, pressed close with murmured thanks; one offered to run ahead for the surgeon, but Hartwell shook his head. "To Pemberley first," said he. "Mr Darcy will send at once for proper aid."

Mary held Turner's hand the whole way back,

answering his broken words with a composure that surprised even herself. When they reached Pemberley, Hartwell drew the carriage to a stop and sprang down, calling softly to a footman who had come out at the sound of wheels. "There has been an accident," he said. "Fetch Mr Darcy at once."

Mary remained within, still holding Turner's hand and speaking gently to keep him calm. A few moments later Darcy appeared at the door, his expression grave but composed. "What has happened?" he asked.

"A fall from a roof," Hartwell replied. "His leg is badly broken, but he bore the journey tolerably."

Darcy gave one brief nod. "Bring him in—carefully. Mrs Reynolds, have a bed made ready in one of the lower rooms, and send for Mr Fletcher at Lambton immediately."

Under his direction the household moved swiftly: Turner was carried inside, the surgeon summoned, and warm blankets fetched. Elizabeth and Georgiana came to assist where they could, while Mary, pale but steady, stood near the fire, watching as order replaced confusion.

When at last the man had been settled and quieted, Darcy turned to them both. "Mr Hartwell, Miss Bennet—Pemberley is obliged to you. Your readiness and good sense have spared this man great suffering."

Hartwell bowed slightly. "Miss Bennet's composure was of more use than my strength, I assure you."

Mary shook her head. "It was your direction, sir, that brought us safely here."

Darcy smiled a little. "Then you were well matched in your offices. I am much obliged to you both." He paused, considering a moment, then added, "If your strength and kindness are not yet exhausted, I would ask another service. Turner's family must be brought hither—they cannot be left alone in such distress. Mrs Reynolds will see that rooms are made ready near his own, for they are likely to remain through Christmas at least."

"Of course," said Hartwell at once. "Miss Bennet and I will go directly."

Mary inclined her head. "It will be a comfort to them to know he is safe."

Darcy nodded his approval. "You will find my groom waiting with a fresh team. Tell Mrs Turner that Pemberley is her home for the present."

As they departed again, Mrs Reynolds came forward with quiet efficiency, already giving orders to prepare the chambers; and Darcy, watching from the door, allowed himself one brief look of satisfaction that his household was equal to both charity and comfort.

The company were still at luncheon when Darcy re-entered. Conversation ceased almost instantly; his countenance, composed but earnest, left no one in doubt that the surgeon had spoken. "Mr Turner will mend," said he, taking his place beside Elizabeth. "The leg is set, and with care he will walk again. But the roof that occasioned his fall must not remain in such a state. To-morrow I mean to go out myself and see it made sound. I know little of thatching, but I shall take one of my men who understands the work. No family in my charge shall be left with the sky for a covering at Christmas."

"My dear Darcy!" cried Bingley, laying down his

napkin with enthusiasm. "Nothing could be better sport than mending a roof with you—though I daresay I shall be more hindrance than help. Still, my hands are at your service; between us, the cottage will soon be tighter than the parson's sermon."

Lady Catherine, who had been partaking of the cold meats with an air of unshakable superiority, raised her brows to their highest pitch. "Fiddlesticks! Gentlemen have no business upon ladders. You will both come to grief for the sake of a tenant who should have mended it himself."

Darcy's tone was mild, but his look carried quiet authority. "Perhaps, madam; but I find the example of good management most convincing when shewn rather than preached."

Elizabeth's eyes met his with quiet pride. "You never fail," said she softly, "to make me love Pemberley better—because you make it kinder."

He looked at her, a shade of warmth crossing his composure. "Then I have succeeded in both my offices—of master and husband."

A murmur of approval ran round the table; the gentlemen in particular seemed caught by his resolution. Colonel Fitzwilliam set down his glass with decision. "If there is a roof to be mended, cousin, you shall not go without your adjutant. I have done rougher work in rougher weather."

St John laughed from farther down the table. "And I'll volunteer as your corporal, sir. My skating this morning has already proved I can keep my balance on treacherous ground."

Hale, ever composed, inclined his head. "If I might

add my services, Mr Darcy, I should be glad to lend both my hands. Nothing restores warmth like honest labour."

Darcy's eyes moved from one to another with quiet pleasure. "Then I shall not lack for either skill or spirit. Between us, the Turners' roof shall be sound again before they return to it."

Wickham—who had hitherto remained silent—spoke with unexpected composure. "If I may, Mr Darcy, I should be glad to assist. I know something of such work, and I would not stand idle when there is need."

For a moment, every eye was turned towards him. Darcy regarded him steadily; the pause that followed seemed to hold both surprise and consideration. At length he said, with grave courtesy, "Your help will be very welcome, Wickham. There is room on the roof for every willing hand."

Lady Catherine, who had begun the conversation in open horror, now found herself confronted with a table of resolute faces. Her sense of propriety yielded to her stronger sense of precedence. "Very well," said she, with lofty resignation, "if gentlemen will so forget themselves, I must commend their motives. Only"—her glance swept down the table—"I hope every gentleman present intends to do his duty by my nephew."

The challenge was unmistakable. Ravenshaw, who had been examining the rim of his glass with philosophical attention, coloured slightly. "Indeed, madam—Mr Darcy—you may command me also. My thoughts, I confess, had been much engaged in pity for the poor fellow's suffering; but such reflections ought rather to quicken one's activity than detain it. I should not wish to be singular in indolence when so many display such ardour for the public good."

A brief silence followed—of that sort which attends a sentiment too fine to be disputed, yet too absurd to be praised.

"I am much obliged to you," said Darcy evenly. "The enterprise will prosper the better for so much good-will."

The tension eased at once; even Lady Catherine, though still visibly unconvinced of the wisdom of the undertaking, could not wholly suppress a look of satisfaction at having regulated the room.

Elizabeth caught her husband's eye. "It seems, Mr Darcy," said she, smiling, "that you have raised a regiment rather than a repair party. I hope the roof is equal to so much zeal."

He returned her look with quiet amusement. "If it is not, it will be by to-morrow night."

"Then," said Elizabeth, turning towards the ladies, "while our champions are abroad in the service of thatch and benevolence, I trust we who remain at home shall not be idle. To-morrow being Christmas Eve, we must see the house properly dressed, and the boxes prepared for the tenants and villagers. I hope we are all equal to the undertaking."

"Indeed we are!" cried Kitty with animation. "I have been longing for an excuse to rob the garden of holly."

"And I," said Georgiana, smiling, "shall count it happiness to help."

Mr Bennet, leaning back in his chair, regarded the

scene with a smile half-ironical, half-pleased. "So order is established at last—Darcy on the roof, and his wife at the helm. I foresee a Christmas conducted with perfect propriety."

Mrs Bennet, beaming, declared, "And with perfect comfort too, for nothing delights me so much as seeing all my children—and their friends—busy and happy together. Only do not forget the mince-pies, Lizzy; no Christmas is complete without them."

Laughter still lingered in the passages when the sound of wheels was heard once more. Mary and Hartwell had returned, bringing with them Turner's wife and children. The little family, weary yet full of gratitude, were received at once by Mrs Reynolds and conducted to the servants' hall, where a bright fire burned and supper waited ready.

Darcy and Elizabeth came presently to see them made comfortable. The mother, with tears of relief, thanked them both for such kindness; her eldest boy stood gazing about the wide kitchen in silent wonder, while the two younger children, perched upon a bench, ate hot stew and fresh bread with unfeigned delight. A footman brought a dish of cold beef and a plate of tarts from the still-room, and Mrs Reynolds herself poured milk for the little ones with a benevolent smile.

Mary, standing beside Hartwell, said softly, "They will rest easier to-night for knowing he is cared for."

"And so shall we," he replied, his tone low but content. "Yet their evening need not end here. There is to be music presently—are we not to practise the hymn for Christmas Night? Would it please you to bring the children?"

Mary's face brightened. "Nothing could be so pleasing."

Accordingly, the little party was soon led to the drawing-room, where Hartwell had taken his place at the pianoforte. The four young ladies—Georgiana, Mary, Kitty, and Anne—stood together near the instrument, their music spread before them, while Mr Hale stood ready with the flute. The lamps were softly shaded, the fire cast a steady glow, and the air seemed already touched with Christmas quiet.

Captain St John sat with the children near the hearth, the youngest upon his knee, speaking to them in soft, cheerful tones as the music began. Hartwell's playing was gentle yet assured, guiding the voices with steady grace. Georgiana's tone was clear and sweet; Mary's joined in earnest harmony; Kitty's lively notes and Anne's shy softness met midway between heaven and hearth, while Mr Hale's flute rose above them like a thread of silver, bright and tender.

When the words came—*Angel of the Holy Night, shining so mild*—the children clasped one another's hands in wonder; and at the threshold, Darcy and Elizabeth, with Jane and Bingley beside them, felt the reverence of it reach them in silence.

When the final chord fell still and the fire crackled softly, one of the children gave a sigh of delight. Darcy looked round the peaceful room and said quietly, "I can imagine no truer hymn to the season." And so the evening closed in perfect harmony, and Pemberley lay hushed in peace and expectation, awaiting Christmas with charity in its deeds and music in its heart.

CHAPTER THE NINTH

"To forgive is the triumph of a noble temper; to deserve forgiveness, its truest reward."

The house was astir as Christmas Eve dawned clear over Pemberley. Fires crackled in the great hearths, garlands waited upon tables to be trimmed, and a cheerful diligence pervaded every passage.

Mrs Bennet, radiant with importance, declared it the happiest day of her life. "Only consider, my dear Lizzy," cried she, "Christmas at Pemberley—with all my daughters about me, and not one of them in want of a new gown! Such felicity does not fall to many mothers."

Elizabeth, amused yet touched, smiled as she helped Mary to fold the cloth for the charitable parcels. "You are right, Mama. It is a day to count blessings—and perhaps to distribute a few."

Lady Catherine, who had taken possession of the largest chair and the nearest fire, surveyed the scene with grave composure. After a moment she said, "Your household is conducted with a propriety that does you credit, Mrs Darcy. There is an air of comfort here that speaks both of care and of command."

Elizabeth looked up, surprised but pleased. "You are very kind, Lady Catherine."

Her ladyship inclined her head with measured approval. "A woman's influence is never so respectable as when directed to the encouragement of order and charity."

"Then I am happy to learn from your example," said Elizabeth, with a smile that mingled gratitude and amusement. "We are soon to carry these parcels into Lambton—may I hope you will accompany us?"

Her ladyship, mollified by the deference, graciously consented.

Mary was already busied with her labels and lists, her expression composed, her manner precise. "One may give unwisely as well as ungenerously," she observed, writing carefully upon a small paper. "Proper distribution is a Christian duty."

Mrs Bennet looked round with a fond sigh. "How industrious she is—exactly like your father when he balances his books! Only do not forget a ribbon or two for prettiness, my dear Mary; charity should be cheerful."

"If I had adorned my books with ribbons," said Mr Bennet placidly, "they might have balanced more prettily—though, I fear, not more exactly."

Elizabeth's eyes danced towards her father, while Jane, ever serene, smiled across the table. "Indeed, Mama, I think every parcel will carry both comfort and good taste."

Meanwhile, the younger ladies had chosen the open air. Georgiana, Kitty, Lydia, and Anne—attended by the Turner children, who chattered in delight—went out into the park to gather holly and ivy for the day's adornment. The sun had brightened the snow till it shone like crystal dust, and their laughter carried lightly through the still air.

"Do not venture too near the slope, Kitty," called Georgiana, as the latter darted towards a hedge bright with berries. "The ground there is uneven beneath the snow."

"I am as sure-footed as any goat upon the hills," cried Kitty merrily—and proved herself mistaken by slipping into a drift and laughing herself upright again.

The Turner children broke into delighted giggles. Lydia's peal of laughter followed. "Oh, Kitty! You would tumble in a ballroom if it pleased you to make a figure!"

"Then I shall take the fall in good humour," Kitty replied, brushing the snow from her cloak, "for no one may be cross upon Christmas Eve."

Even Anne's gentle reserve gave way to laughter, and the cheerful sound echoed among the trees.

When they returned with their baskets—laden with holly, ivy, bay, and laurel—the great hall was transformed into a scene of ordered bustle. Elizabeth, Jane, and Caroline had set the tables for sorting and wrapping, while Mrs Bennet went from one end of the room to the other, extolling every arrangement as "truly genteel."

While they were thus employed, Darcy entered, already dressed for out-of-doors. His expression bore that quiet satisfaction which always attended him when duty and good humour met.

"Bingley, Fitzwilliam, and the others are ready," said he, drawing on his gloves. "We mean to see the Turner roof made sound before dusk—and to have the Yule-log brought in before nightfall."

Elizabeth looked up from her work. "Then I hope you will not return frozen."

"Only refreshed," he replied with a smile. "There is

no better exercise than service."

Lady Catherine, whose attention had turned from ribbons to resolution, said sharply, "I trust you have proper assistance, Darcy. Gentlemen upon ladders are a sight I detest."

Darcy bowed slightly. "You may depend upon me, Aunt. One of my men will shew us what to do, and I believe even Mr Hale may be equal to a mallet."

"Equal—and eager," said Hale from the doorway. "The frost promises a fine day for building roofs and reputations alike."

Mr Bennet looked up from his chair with mild irony. "I have always found that a gentleman upon a ladder is less alarming than a lady upon a principle."

A murmur of amusement ran round the room; even Elizabeth's eyes sparkled. Fitzwilliam, with his usual good humour, came to the rescue. "Then we shall endeavour to be as unalarming as possible, sir."

Caroline, arranging a bough of holly upon the mantel and trimming its ribbon to fall just so, looked at him with quiet admiration. She had often studied conversation as an art, yet seldom seen it employed with such ease and benevolence. For a moment she wished she possessed the power of soothing where others might offend, and resolved that she would learn it if she could. Fitzwilliam caught her glance and returned it with a smile—so natural, so kind, that it left her wondering whether the lesson had already begun.

"Come, gentlemen," cried Bingley, laughing. "Let us all acquire consequence in carpentry! If we linger much longer, Lady Catherine will have us under arrest before we reach the door."

"Indeed she will," said her ladyship; but she spoke too late. The gentlemen were already gathering their coats, while Darcy's foreman had the tools laid in a wagon ready for departure.

Outside, the sound of wheels and cheerful voices echoed across the courtyard. First went the estate wagon, the foreman at the reins. Next came Darcy's phaeton, driven by himself, with Colonel Fitzwilliam beside him; the horses stepped briskly in the frosty air. Following them rolled the barouche, conveying Bingley, Hale, Hartwell, and Wickham, while St John—declaring himself born for adventure—sprang lightly up beside the coachman. Last rode Ravenshaw on horseback, keeping a genteel distance, yet plainly resolved to appear part of the enterprise.

From the windows, the ladies watched them depart. Mrs Bennet clasped her hands with maternal pride. "What a delightful sight—so many gentlemen off to do good! Christmas, I am sure, was invented for the improvement of men."

"Yes," said Mr Bennet. "I feel myself a better man already, and without the trouble of a mallet."

The hours passed in cheerful exertion. Within doors, the great hall became a scene of pleasant confusion: baskets and ribbons, brown paper and sprigs of evergreen in every corner, laughter and exclamations in every tone. Mrs Bennet directed the business with a zeal that delighted even Elizabeth, who had not often seen her mother so truly happy.

"Only look, my dear Lizzy," cried she, holding up a parcel tied with red cord. "A loaf, a bit of beef, and a plum-pudding for every family! I declare, Pemberley shall be blessed for a hundred years to come."

"And perhaps," said Elizabeth, smiling, "it will remember that the blessing began with you."

"La, child! It began with your good Mr Darcy and his fortune—but I am content to assist."

Jane, ever the peacemaker, added a ribbon to each parcel "for prettiness," as her mother had urged. Mary, who had begun by questioning whether ribbons properly belonged to virtue, was soon persuaded that they might adorn it without offence. Even Lady Catherine deigned to pronounce that "good order had at last been introduced into benevolence."

By mid-day the tables were covered with neat rows of parcels ready for delivery, and the married ladies prepared to set out in the Pemberley carriage, while the younger ones remained to decorate the house.

At the Turner cottage, meanwhile, the air rang with the thud of mallets, the rustle of straw, and voices raised in good humour. Under the direction of Darcy's foreman, who shewed them where each bundle must lie, the work went forward briskly. Darcy, coat discarded, stood upon a ladder beside the low thatched roof; Fitzwilliam and Hale steadied the new frame below, while Wickham and St John, side by side, vied in cheerful rivalry—each striking with such vigour that the foreman at last declared the roof would outlast them both. Their laughter was as frequent as their blows, yet the thatch rose trim and true beneath their hands.

"You have a steady hand, Wickham," said Darcy. "I did not know the army taught such craftsmanship."

"The army taught little beyond endurance," Wickham replied with a faint smile. "But a soldier who would keep his quarters dry must learn something of roofs."

"And of character too," said Fitzwilliam, settling the straw with the air of a man determined to make it behave.

Hartwell, working beside Hale, laughed good-humouredly. "Then your regiment, Wickham, was a better school than half the universities in England."

Ravenshaw, standing at a respectful distance, had begun with commendable zeal, but soon found occasion to admire rather than assist. After a few minutes' effort he paused to examine his glove and declared, with a pained air, "A pity my arm was strained last week, else I should rival even Mr Wickham in industry."

Bingley, unwilling to let embarrassment disturb good humour, said pleasantly, "Then your judgment shall make amends for your labour, Ravenshaw. We shall count upon you to tell us when the roof looks sound enough to please the ladies."

The work advanced rapidly under such discipline, and by early afternoon the roof stood firm and sound against the winter sky. When all was complete, the men drew back a little to survey their handiwork; and Darcy, well pleased, declared himself satisfied.

As the company reached for their coats, Wickham found himself beside Darcy and said in a low voice, "I have not forgotten, Mr Darcy, how much I once misused your forbearance. I squandered your generosity and made free with your honour where I ought only to have guarded it. I cannot undo the past; I can only confess it, and beg leave to prove, by conduct henceforth, that repentance need not be idle. If you cannot forgive, I must submit; but if you can, I shall hold it as the greatest act of friendship ever extended to me."

Darcy looked at him steadily; surprise softened into gravity, then into something gentler still. "I do believe you," he said at last. "Let us both prove it—each in his way."

Wickham inclined his head, unable to speak further. There was no triumph in his countenance—only the quiet release of a man who, having long borne a burden, had at last set it down.

Within Pemberley, the charitable party had returned glowing from their rounds. The sight of the villagers' delight—especially the children's—had brightened every heart. Mrs Bennet declared it the very thing to make Christmas respectable; Lady Catherine pronounced the organisation faultless, though she took to herself the credit of its system.

The younger ladies, under Caroline's direction and with much joy and laughter, had meanwhile transformed the house. Garlands of holly twined about the stair and gallery; clusters of ivy hung between the windows; and the great chandelier sparkled with scarlet berries. Anne, who had never before assisted in so cheerful a labour, looked about her with quiet wonder.

"It is all so different from Rosings," she said softly to Georgiana. "One could almost imagine the season invented for happiness."

"Perhaps it was," Georgiana replied, smiling. "At least, Pemberley believes so."

When the men returned at last, the daylight was

fading; their boots were white with snow, their faces ruddy from the cold, and the cheerful sound of their voices preceded them into the hall. Cloaks were shaken out, gloves pulled off, and every man had his tale to tell. Darcy spoke of the roof made tight against the weather; Fitzwilliam laughed over St John's zeal in trimming the thatch; Bingley declared that Hale's patience had saved them all from ruin; and Wickham—blushing a little at the general praise—owned that he had not handled a tool so usefully since boyhood. Even Ravenshaw was commended for his judgment in pronouncing the work complete at precisely the right moment.

The ladies, who had gathered to greet them, were not to be outdone in achievement. Elizabeth reported that every parcel had been delivered, Jane that each family had received both comfort and cheer, and Mary, with quiet satisfaction, observed that charity, when rightly bestowed, blesses the giver no less than the receiver. Mrs Bennet, beaming, declared that all her daughters had done her credit. Caroline added with feeling, "And if beauty and charity may be joined, I think we have contrived both. Pemberley has never felt more fit for Christmas."

Fitzwilliam's eyes rested on her with an expression of regard, as if the sentiment had disclosed more heart than he had ever before suspected. Caroline, meeting his gaze by chance, coloured slightly and turned again to the fire, uncertain whether she was more pleased or astonished to have earned it.

The cheerful company soon began to part for their rooms to dress for dinner. Cloaks and gloves were carried off, garlands straightened, and the great hall—

so lately alive with voices—sank into a contented hush.

Anne, lingering behind in the pleasant after-feeling of the day's merriment, paused in the gallery where a wreath of holly hung loosely from its nail. The corridor lay still; the lamps were newly lit, and through the casement panes the soft fall of fresh Christmas snow seemed to deepen the quiet. As she reached to secure the wreath, a voice—smooth and low—sounded just behind her.

"Miss de Bourgh—how fortunate that I meet you here. I had feared the day would end without one word from you."

She turned, startled, to see Ravenshaw approaching with that composed air which always seemed meant for an audience.

"I am glad," he continued, "to find that even the severest winter can soften its heart at Pemberley. You look—if I may be permitted to say so—quite in harmony with the season."

Anne coloured faintly, uncertain whether to withdraw or reply. "You are very obliging, sir."

"Not obliging—sincere," said he, stepping nearer. "I observed you this morning among the holly-gatherers. I never saw the frost so willing to yield its beauty."

She looked down, confused but not displeased. "You praise trifles, Mr Ravenshaw."

"Then let me praise them where they are deserved," he returned, lowering his voice. "I have resolved that, when the ball is held on St Stephen's Night, the first dance shall be mine—if you will do me that honour."

Anne, wholly unprepared for such a speech, hesitated; surprise and timid gratification contended upon her face. Before she could answer, the sound of steps echoed along the corridor.

Ravenshaw straightened, his expression instantly composed. Wickham appeared at the end of the passage, his glance passing coolly from one to the other before he bowed and slowly moved on.

"I believe we are called to dinner," said Ravenshaw, recovering his smoothness. "May I hope your answer will not disappoint me?"

Anne managed a small smile. "I—shall not forget what you have said, sir."

"Then I am content," he replied, bowing low before withdrawing down the gallery.

She remained a moment where she stood, her hand resting on the holly-branch, her heart beating faster than she knew why.

After dinner, the household assembled again in the great hall, brilliant with candle-light and fragrant with evergreen. Conversation rose in cheerful bursts, mingled with the rustle of gowns and the crackle of the fire. Darcy gave quiet directions to the servants. "Now then—let us see the Yule-log in its place."

The great doors were opened, and the log—seasoned oak bound in ivy—was borne in by two footmen to a murmur of applause.

"'Tis prodigious!" cried Mrs Bennet. "I declare, Lizzy, it will burn till Easter."

"Then we are secured against all chill and misfortune," said Elizabeth, smiling as Darcy laid the first touch of flame.

Jane added softly, "And against all dull spirits, I think."

"Very proper, Nephew," said Lady Catherine, with stately satisfaction. "I have ever maintained that a good Yule-log is the very basis of Christmas comfort."

"And what comfort," said Fitzwilliam, smiling, "could surpass that of being here, in this hall, among such friends as these?"

The blaze caught at once, leaping bright upon the polished floor. Kitty clapped her hands. "How merry it looks! May we sit up till it burns through, Lizzy?"

"Not unless you mean to greet Christmas morning in your shawl," Elizabeth laughed.

Bingley, standing beside Jane, said with fond admiration, "Let her—there can be no finer celebration than keeping watch beside so noble a fire."

Mrs Bennet smiled about her with fond complacency. "Such comfort and cheer—it is quite everything I could wish for my family."

Across the hearth, Fitzwilliam turned to Caroline, his manner shewing that her exertions in the day's adornments had not escaped his notice. "Miss Bingley," said he, with pleasant seriousness, "you have contrived to make this room fit for a queen."

She looked up, startled but pleased. "You are very good, Colonel. I only tied the bows; the greenery did all the rest."

"Then you must allow me to say the bows improved it," he returned, with a smile that sent a quick flush to her cheek.

Ravenshaw, meanwhile, attended Lady Catherine with practised devotion. "Your ladyship's direction in taste is apparent in every bough," said he smoothly.

Lady Catherine inclined her head, well satisfied. "I

flatter myself my judgement has not decayed."

Anne, seated beside her mother, coloured faintly at his tone; but when he turned the conversation towards her—inquiring whether she had found the morning's air invigorating—she answered with quiet civility that surprised even herself.

At that moment Darcy beckoned to Mrs Reynolds. "It grows late, yet there is one more guest we must receive."

A brief whisper passed among the company as the housekeeper returned with Mrs Turner and her children. The little family hesitated at the threshold until Elizabeth went forward with an encouraging smile. "Pray come in, Mrs Turner. We could not end Christmas Eve without those who have most shared it."

Mrs Turner curtsied low. "Madam, we owe you everything—Mr Darcy, you and the gentlemen have given us our home again."

Darcy shook his head. "You owe us nothing but your good cheer. That is payment enough."

The eldest boy gazed round in awe. "Please, sir—is that the King's fire?"

A gentle laugh passed through the room. "Not quite," said Darcy, "though I hope it burns as faithfully."

At Elizabeth's request, Hartwell stepped forward, Bible in hand. "Shall we read?" he asked quietly.

"If you please," said Darcy; and the room fell still.

Hartwell read the verses of the shepherds keeping watch, his voice steady and devout. When he ceased, Georgiana softly began the carols. Mary, Kitty, and Anne joined their voices to hers; others followed, until the whole hall was filled with gentle harmony.

Mrs Bennet dabbed her eyes. "How heavenly they sound—just like the angels themselves!"

Even Lady Catherine, subdued, murmured, "Very well chosen—quite suitable to the occasion."

When the carols ended, Darcy stepped forward. "Thank you, my friends. May peace dwell with every heart here to-night." He nodded to Mrs Reynolds, who led the Turners away with warm farewells.

As the doors closed softly, Elizabeth turned to her husband, smiling through the glow. "It has been a good day."

"The best of all," he replied.

Her hand found his upon the chair beside her. The fire crackled; the Yule-log burned steady and bright; and within that quiet splendour, Pemberley kept its Christmas in perfect peace.

CHAPTER THE TENTH

"Happiness does not depend upon splendour, but upon those who share it."

Christmas morning brought a light so pure it seemed to hush the very air. Fresh snow covered the hills and terraces like linen newly pressed, and the great house stood serene amid its woods, smoke rising straight from every chimney. Within, warmth and merriment had already begun—the pleasant confusion of a household waking to joy, and the quick laughter of servants exchanging 'Happy Christmas,' and good-will seemed to meet at every threshold.

In the breakfast-parlour the company assembled by cheerful degrees, all bright faces and pleasant disorder. Elizabeth, whose countenance spoke a happiness beyond ceremony, moved among her guests with easy grace, welcoming each new arrival as if the day had been contrived for their particular pleasure. Mrs Bennet entered all smiles, declaring, "A happy Christmas to you all!" in a tone of such hearty delight that the greeting was instantly returned from every side.

Before the tea was poured, Darcy drew Elizabeth quietly towards the hearth. "I fear," said he, "that in so large a household your own writing-instruments have been borrowed past all endurance. You must allow me to supply their place." He placed in her hands a small box of polished wood; within lay a neat array of silver-trimmed quills and a cut-glass inkstand.

Elizabeth's eyes sparkled. "You will repent it, sir, when I employ them to correct your accounts—or to instruct your steward."

"I shall risk it," he replied, smiling. "A husband may forgive a great deal when the handwriting is his wife's."

Her look was answer enough, and they rejoined the others with that quiet understanding which marked their best companionship.

Bingley, meanwhile, could not wait another minute. "Jane, my dearest, you must open this at once—it is the smallest thing in the world, yet it has been tormenting my patience since breakfast was announced." He set upon her lap a parcel wrapped in tissue. She unfolded it and drew out a shawl of fine wool, its border delicately worked in pale blue.

"Oh, Charles—how beautiful it is!"

"I only hope it keeps you warmer than all the compliments you deserve," cried he, his eyes dancing. "If there is a princess in England fairer than my wife, I have yet to meet her."

Mrs Bennet, at the other end of the table, exclaimed that she had always said as much, and that no man living had ever chosen so well.

Lydia's voice soon followed. "Look what I have got! A bonnet—and new ribbons too! Mr Wickham says I may trim it as I please." She held it aloft with unfeigned delight.

Her husband, modestly pleased, said only, "I feared to spoil it by guessing your taste; it seemed safest to leave genius to its own invention."

"Genius!" cried Lydia, laughing. "You have learnt to say very pretty things, sir."

Even Mr Bennet allowed that this was the happiest of Christmas mornings; and, in a fit of unusual gallantry, he presented his wife with a small mirror in a carved case, accompanied by a bottle of lavender-water—"to revive your spirits," as he said, "whenever felicity should overcome your nerves; and to remind you that you are still the handsomest among us."

Mrs Bennet received it with rapture, declaring him the best of husbands, and pronouncing the gift the most elegant and considerate imaginable. Mr Bennet, satisfied with the success of his raillery, retreated behind his newspaper with an expression of contentment that almost amounted to good humour.

The table grew lively with greetings and plans. The St Stephen's Ball furnished subject enough for Lydia and Kitty, while Mary and Hartwell spoke quietly of the hymns to be sung at church.

Lady Catherine, seated in state at the upper end, surveyed the cheerful company with complacent dignity. "Colonel Fitzwilliam," said she presently, "you will attend me to the service. Anne and I shall require your escort."

Ravenshaw, ever alert for opportunity, leaned forward with an air of respectful eagerness. "Should your ladyship wish for an additional attendant, I shall count it my honour to be of service."

Her ladyship regarded him a moment, as if weighing the propriety of the offer; at length she inclined her head with stately approval. "Very well, Mr Ravenshaw; that is handsomely said. Colonel Fitzwilliam will then do wisely to attend Miss Bingley—thus the company is best accommodated. Arrangements are always more agreeable when made with due consideration."

The Colonel's brow lifted scarcely a line, but his glance towards Darcy betrayed a moment's surprise. Mr Darcy's own expression altered very little, though his silence had in it something more than indifference. He seemed to observe Mr Ravenshaw as one might a man testing limits not wholly his own.

By the time breakfast was concluded the carriages stood ready. The household gathered in the great hall, all good humour and bustle—cloaks adjusted, mufflers tied. The younger party—Kitty, Georgiana, Anne, St John, and Hale—ventured out laughing into the snow, while the older guests arranged themselves with more decorum. Mrs Reynolds had undertaken to see that Turner's wife and children were comfortably conveyed; the little ones, well wrapped and eager, were soon settled, their laughter mingling with the general cheer.

The road to the village wound bright through the trees, every branch glittering with frost. As they approached the church, the bell began to ring—clear and steady over the hills. Villagers turned to wave as the Pemberley party alighted; some of the children ran forward to shew their Sunday best, and the ladies stooped to praise their new ribbons.

One of the boys darted up behind St John, gave him a playful poke, and cried, "You are touched, sir!" St John burst out laughing and gave chase, pursuing several of the culprits round the churchyard with mock determination, declaring them all far too quick for him.

"Catch them, Captain!—do not let them beat you so easily!" cried Kitty, laughing till her cheeks were pink.

The girls clapped and called encouragement until

Elizabeth, smiling but resolute, reminded them that they should be late for the service if the game continued.

Within the little church the air was sweet with evergreens and candle-wax. The pews filled quickly, gentry and tenants mingling with unaffected good-will. The vicar gave a short, earnest discourse on peace and charity; and, when he concluded, invited Mr Hartwell to speak.

Hartwell rose with calm composure and read a few lines from the Gospel of Luke: "Glory to God in the highest, and on earth peace, good-will toward men." He paused, then added, in a voice both kind and sincere, "There are few words more familiar to us, yet few that ask more of the heart. Peace does not descend because the world is still, but because forgiveness is alive within it. If we would honour this day aright, let our praise be shewn in gentleness one towards another, and in good-will that is not spent with the season."

Mary Bennet's eyes shone with quiet pride.

A brief silence followed, as though every heart had paused to take the measure of the words. At the vicar's nod, the choir began—clear, steady voices rising from the little gallery; the children's bright tones mingled with those of their elders until the whole congregation joined. The music was simple, yet full of heart; and many recalled that its harmony was owing to Mr Hartwell's patient care and Miss Mary Bennet's good judgement. Even Mr Bennet was heard to declare the arrangement "sensible and unpretending," and no one chose to dispute it.

When the final verse faded and the people filed out

into the winter sunshine, there was laughter on the steps, and warmth enough in every breast to make even the coldest day a happy one. While Lydia spoke cheerfully with Mary and Kitty, Wickham approached Hartwell. "Sir," he began, humble yet earnest, "as one much in need of forgiveness, your words were a comfort to me. I do not deserve it; but it is a treasure my heart longs to find."

Hartwell's look was one of quiet compassion. "Then take courage, Mr Wickham. Remember Him who has graven us upon the palms of His hands; for though we forget in our weakness, He does not forget."

Serious reflection yielded, as it generally must, to the more cheerful duties of civilities and farewells; and Lady Catherine was soon surrounded by bows and curtsies, which she accepted with that composed condescension long familiar to her acquaintance.

Ravenshaw, having secured his place at her side, offered his arm to Miss de Bourgh; yet, as they descended the church steps, he bent his head and said, low enough that her ladyship could not overhear, "I hope, Miss de Bourgh, that you have not forgotten our little engagement for the first set at to-morrow's ball. I should count it the happiest privilege of the season."

Anne coloured, glanced timidly towards her mother, and murmured that she could not promise—but she smiled as she said it, which was promise enough for him.

Mr Darcy, who stood a little apart, observed the exchange with more concern than surprise. Ravenshaw's attentions had already engaged his notice, and though suspicion stirred within him, he judged it prudent to be silent—for the present.

A few paces behind, Colonel Fitzwilliam offered his hand to Caroline as they crossed a patch of ice. "You advance fearlessly, Miss Bingley; I begin to suspect Derbyshire's winters hold no terrors for you."

"Not while they provide such gallant assistance, Colonel," she returned with composure, though her eyes betrayed amusement.

Georgiana had fallen a little behind with Hale. They walked slowly, watching the carriages gather and the villagers disperse in cheerful knots along the path.

"The service was very affecting," she said softly. "I liked Mr Hartwell's words about peace being alive within forgiveness."

Hale inclined his head. "Indeed—and if I may say so without offence, I think Pemberley itself has proved them. Pray forgive me if I speak too plainly, but I have heard reports—idle perhaps—of Mr Wickham's former conduct towards your family and the Bennets. It seems to me no household could shew greater charity than yours has done in receiving him again with such civility."

Georgiana coloured a little, but her voice was calm. "You are very good to think so. We have all been wronged, in one way or another; yet we are none the poorer for forgiving."

Hale regarded her with quiet admiration. "Then I think, Miss Darcy, that Pemberley keeps the truest Christmas of all."

Her eyes brightened, and she answered only with a smile; but it was one that might have warmed even the coldest morning.

Darcy and Elizabeth found the Bingleys and Bennets gathered near the gate, waiting while the carriages drew round. Jane's face glowed with contentment; Bingley was exclaiming that he had never heard a service so cheerful in his life.

"Everything at Pemberley is cheerful," declared Mrs Bennet, beaming. "Even the sermon sounded as if it had been written expressly for our family."

Mr Bennet smiled. "Then let us be thankful it was not longer, my dear; or we might have found our virtues too well examined."

Elizabeth laughed. "Papa, you cannot deny you were pleased to hear so many good resolutions at once."

"I am always pleased to hear them," he replied with his accustomed composure. "It is only their fulfilment that alarms me."

Bingley turned to Darcy with his usual warmth. "I believe, Darcy, the vicar has made us all better men— at least until dinner."

"Then dinner must not be delayed," said Darcy, smiling. "We shall hope to preserve our virtue through the pudding."

There was general laughter as the company moved towards the waiting carriages, the air bright with sunshine and good humour. Christmas Day at Pemberley had begun as it ought—with harmony within and good-will without.

By evening the house had settled into that gentle hush which succeeds a day of gladness. The candles were newly lighted, the fires replenished, and a softened cheer pervaded every room. After dinner, Elizabeth persuaded those servants still on duty to join the family in the great drawing-room for a little music, that all might share alike in the closing comfort of the day.

At her request, Mrs Reynolds had brought in Turner's wife and children, their faces bright with expectation; and soon two footmen appeared, carrying Turner himself in a wheeled chair, warmly wrapped and smiling at the sight before him. His entrance drew a low stir of sympathy and welcome from every side. Darcy went forward at once to greet him, while Elizabeth saw him placed near the fire, where he might best enjoy the music. She thought there could be no truer picture of Christmas than this gathering of high and low about the same hearth, united by good-will and gratitude.

When all were settled, Georgiana stepped forward a little, her composure gentle but firm. "If you please," said she, "I should like to offer a small piece I have written. My friends have been so kind as to perform it with me. It is called *Angel of the Holy Night*."

A quiet murmur of approval ran through the company. Hartwell took his place at the pianoforte, Hale beside him with the flute. Georgiana, Mary, Kitty, and Anne stood together, their music in hand. When Hartwell struck the first low chords, all other sounds seemed to fade; the melody rose clear and pure, Hale's flute winding softly between the verses.

Angel of the holy night,
Shining so mild;
Guiding the shepherds' hearts,
Seeking the Child.
Peace on the earth below,
Mercy's pure light;

All hearts shall worship Him—
Love's holy Light.

The voices blended sweetly—Georgiana's clear tone leading, Mary's steadier note supporting, Kitty's light soprano brightening the edge, and Anne's timid but earnest voice trembling through the harmony. When they began the second verse, even the smallest child seemed spell-bound.

Cradle so lowly laid,
Manger of hay;
Glory of heav'nly hosts
Hail Him this day.
Glory to God on high,
Grace shining bright;
Sing we, Emmanuel—
Love's holy Light.

The last line was repeated softly, the flute sustaining the note until it died away. For a moment there was only the crackle of the fire and the faint breath of candles. Then the applause came—gentle, heartfelt, universal. Mrs Bennet declared it the prettiest thing she had ever heard; Mrs Reynolds wiped her eyes; even Lady Catherine pronounced it "sensible and becoming," and wished that more modern compositions would shew such modest taste.

Turner said in a low, feeling voice, "It was worth the pain, madam, only to hear that once." Elizabeth bent to thank him, her own eyes bright.

Darcy, standing near the hearth where all could see

him, soon commanded the company's attention. "My friends," said he, "this house has known many Christmases, yet I do not think it has seen one more truly blessed than to-day. We have been favoured with health, with peace, and with one another's company; and I cannot let the night close without thanking you for the kindness and good-will which have filled it. May the spirit that has guided us through this day abide with us through the year; and may every hearth represented here be as warm and happy as this one. A very happy Christmas to you all."

There were gentle murmurs of "and to you, Mr Darcy," as the room stirred again. The servants withdrew with many grateful smiles, and Mrs Reynolds led the Turners quietly out. Turner, expressing his gratitude to have his family included, declared it one of the happiest Christmases they had ever known.

When the doors had closed, a pleasant hum of conversation arose among the remaining guests. Lydia, flushed with happiness and unwilling to be silent long, caught her husband's eye with a look of irrepressible glee.

Wickham, smiling, rose from his seat. "If I may trespass a moment longer upon your patience," said he, "Mrs Wickham and I have a little news which we hope will be received in the same spirit of good-will that has marked this day. Before the next Christmas comes, we expect—God willing—to be three instead of two."

A murmur of surprise and pleasure ran through the room. Mrs Bennet, quite overcome, declared that she had always said her Lydia would be the first to make her a grandmother; and her daughters, gathering round their sister in affectionate delight, seemed for once entirely united in joy. Darcy, Bingley, and even Mr Bennet each shook Wickham by the hand; the warmth of the moment left no trace of former discord behind.

Amid the cheer, Ravenshaw drew near and bowed towards Anne. "Miss de Bourgh," said he, in a tone low and deferential, "you sang to-night as angels must—so softly that one could scarcely tell whether the sound came from earth or heaven."

Anne coloured deeply and looked down at her music. "You are very good, sir," she murmured, scarcely above a whisper.

Her mother, hearing him, said with importance, "Anne has always possessed a delicate voice, though it has never been properly cultivated."

Ravenshaw smiled. "It is so natural, madam, it can need no cultivation at all."

Lady Catherine returned the smile with the complacency of one who sees her daughter's merit at length universally acknowledged.

From across the room, Caroline observed the little scene. Anne's look of shy pleasure and Ravenshaw's deferential bow betrayed nothing that could offend propriety—only an earnestness in his manner, and a warmth upon her cheek that spoke too plainly. Caroline felt discomposed by the sight, and, unwilling to trust her countenance, turned away and joined her brother with a composure that did not come easily.

The hour grew late. The fire sank low; the candlelight cast a mellow gleam upon garlands and gilt frames, while the company lingered, unwilling to let the day depart. At length Elizabeth rose, her eyes alight with merriment, and declared that Christmas must at last surrender to St Stephen's—"for if we mean to dance to-morrow, we must begin the day before it escapes us altogether!"

Anne, following her mother upstairs, looked back for a moment towards the darkened drawing-room, her thoughts full of the kindness she had received and the gentleness with which it had been offered.

So Christmas Night at Pemberley closed—in comfort, harmony, and good-will; though with the faintest shadow lying unseen among them.

CHAPTER THE ELEVENTH

"Every family must have its occasion for wonder; the best are those which end in affection."

The conversation at dinner on St Stephen's Day would scarcely fix upon any subject but the ball. Every topic, however begun—dress, music, partners, or arrangements—was sure to end there; and the cheerful bustle of preparation gave animation to every countenance.

Captain St John, seated beside Kitty, bent towards her with an air of mock formality. "Miss Bennet," said he, "since all the world means to dance to-night, may I hope to be remembered among your engagements? I should count it a singular honour if you would bestow on me the first two sets."

Kitty coloured and laughed. "You will be disappointed, Captain; I am but a middling dancer, and shall disgrace your gallantry."

"Then I am doubly bound to insist," he returned, smiling. "I would rather stand up with cheerful imperfection than mope in solitary excellence."

Ravenshaw, who had contrived to place himself beside Anne, said with courteous solicitude, "I trust you are not over-fatigued by yesterday's festivities, Miss de Bourgh. Pemberley would be far less bright this evening were you to deny us your share in the dancing."

Anne coloured faintly and replied that she had every intention of joining the company.

"Then I am fortunate indeed," he said, lowering his voice just enough for her to catch it. "I have a claim upon your first set, you remember."

Georgiana looked up with a smile, guessing no more than simple courtesy in the exchange. Lady Catherine, who had been discoursing upon the proper arrangement of the musicians, caught the last of his speech and interposed with authority. "Anne will dance, certainly; but she must not over-exert herself. There is nothing so ungraceful as fatigue. You shall wear the new gown of pale green, my dear; it is a shade of perfect distinction, and the sleeves are not unbecoming." At this, Anne looked pleased.

Bingley declared he had never yet seen a green gown that did not flatter every lady who wore it; whereupon Jane laughed, and said she hoped the company would not appear entirely in that colour, or poor Mr Bingley would be at a loss which partner to admire.

"I shall not wear green, I assure you," cried Lydia from farther down the table. "I am to be in blue—and Wickham shall match me, for I told him he must look lively, and he promised he would. There is nothing so dull as a room full of black coats; I dare say every eye will be upon us!"

Kitty protested that she would not stand near her sister, lest she be quite outshone; upon which Captain St John declared that he would appear in full uniform— "for," said he, "somebody must represent the regiment, since all the best men are gone over to domestic service."

Colonel Fitzwilliam, smiling, added that he might do the same, "though my coat has seen more dinners than campaigns."

Wickham laughed. "Then I shall be safe among heroes; for my own plain coat will never compete with such gallantry."

The easy mirth that followed restored the table to perfect cheerfulness.

Elizabeth smiled. "Pemberley will have little difficulty in appearing cheerful this evening, I think, when such lively spirits preside at the table."

Darcy's glance met hers—steady and approving—and enough to say that he found her observation perfectly just.

"Indeed," said Mr Bennet good-humouredly, "I do not recollect seeing so many happy faces in one room since your wedding-day, Lizzy."

Mrs Bennet, glowing with satisfaction, declared that nothing could be more delightful than to see so many fine gentlemen assembled for her daughters to dance with. "It is quite a comfort," she added, "to know they will not be at a loss for partners."

Thus the dinner passed with uncommon animation—Lady Catherine issuing instructions, Mrs Bennet issuing blessings, and the younger party full of spirits and expectation, as if every smile were already half a dance begun.

By seven o'clock the winter dusk had deepened, and a pleasant stir of anticipation pervaded the house. Servants passed briskly with candles and coal-scuttles; Mrs Reynolds gave her last directions that the great-hall fires be mended and the sconces newly trimmed. From the gallery above came the faint strains of tuning instruments—the musicians from Lambton had arrived, and were arranging their music.

The gentlemen, already dressed, had gathered in the library, while the ladies withdrew to their rooms to prepare. Soon the sound of wheels crunched over the snow, and lights appeared among the trees. Within, the air grew bright with candle-glow reflected in gilt mirrors; every polished surface seemed to multiply the cheer. The great staircase filled with soft voices, rustling silk, and the fragrance of fresh garlands.

Elizabeth, descending arm-in-arm with Jane, found the hall already lively with arrivals—neighbours from Lambton and Kympton, the Gouldings from Matlock, and half a dozen families whom Darcy had long wished to repay with Pemberley's hospitality. Lady Catherine was stationed near the entrance, bestowing condescensions with impressive punctuality, while Mr Bennet looked on from a safe distance, amused by the ceremony of introductions.

Darcy welcomed each guest with unhurried civility, his manner perfectly composed. "You have contrived a very pretty evening, my dear," Elizabeth whispered as she passed him; to which he replied, "It is you, madam, who have contrived it—Pemberley has not looked so well since its first Christmas."

At eight o'clock the musicians struck the first notes of a country-dance, and the scene became one of brilliant animation. The lamps blazed, the mirrors shone, and the floor filled rapidly. Darcy led out Elizabeth for the first couple; Bingley, all cheerfulness, stood up with his Jane; and Wickham took his place with Lydia, who could scarcely contain her delight at being so attended.

Fitzwilliam led out Miss Bingley with practised ease; St John stood opposite Kitty, whose laughter might be heard even through the music; and Hale persuaded Miss Darcy, a little timid at first, to take her place with quiet grace. Hartwell, arriving a moment later, requested a lower place in the same set with Miss Mary Bennet, and she—after a modest hesitation—accepted.

Ravenshaw, having kept his word, approached Anne with a bow of easy grace. "You must allow me to say, Miss de Bourgh, that your gown becomes you to perfection. Your lady mother has chosen with her usual discernment." He paused, as if to enjoy the effect of his words, and smiled when he saw her colour rise.

Anne inclined her head modestly. "My mother is so good as to think the shade becoming," she said, her voice scarcely above the music.

"And she was perfectly right," returned Ravenshaw. "It is a rare pleasure to see taste and grace so happily united. The moment, I believe, is mine." He extended his hand with gallant assurance.

She hesitated only a second longer before taking it; her step, though cautious, was light, and the unusual attention she attracted lent her a new animation.

As the dance progressed, Caroline, moving through the figures with Fitzwilliam, could not help but notice Anne and Ravenshaw a few sets away. Each time the line brought her round, she caught some new glimpse of Anne's soft colour and shy smile, and of Ravenshaw's attentive air that seemed, to a discerning eye, a little too practised.

Wickham, engaged with Lydia in the same dance, marked it too in the intervals between the figures. His expression was thoughtful—almost grave—for he, of all men, knew how easily courtesy might serve as disguise.

Lady Catherine, however, beheld the scene with perfect satisfaction. "Anne dances uncommonly well this evening," she announced to no one in particular. "It is the effect of air and exercise. I have long maintained that a change of air is essential to her spirits."

As the first set concluded, the company broke into cheerful conversation, and Elizabeth's heart was full. Pemberley, bright with music and good-will, seemed to her the very image of contentment. Yet, at the far end of the hall, near the long windows, Ravenshaw had already bent once more towards Anne, his tone so low and earnest that even Georgiana, passing with Hale, could not catch his words.

When the second dance began, and the press and warmth of the hall grew considerable, Anne—overcome by the heat—readily accepted Ravenshaw's suggestion to step into the adjoining parlour for a little air.

He led her to a chair. "The company grows oppressive," said he, in a lowered tone. "I fear this room is too small for so much beauty; still, the air is less crowded, and may suit you better."

Anne tried to smile. "You are very kind, sir; I only need to catch my breath."

He inclined his head, all solicitude. "Then the air will serve us here. Pemberley loses nothing by a moment's rest, when its brightest ornament remains in view." He paused, watching her colour deepen. "I have seldom met with a disposition so gentle, nor one that seems to wish so little for itself. I would wager you have not been permitted to know how much liberty might become you."

"Liberty, sir?"

"Independence," he said softly. "The freedom to choose one's own happiness—to move, to live, to love as the heart inclines. You would shine in such a life. You were made to command admiration, not to sit silent under another's direction."

The compliment, though artfully disguised as sympathy, startled her. She turned slightly away. "My health does not always permit such—activity."

"Your health," he replied, "would improve with spirit; and your spirit with freedom. Believe me, Miss de Bourgh, you have every right to seek it. There are men—some in this very room—who would give all they possess to see you mistress of your own fortune."

Anne's colour deepened. The sudden mention of fortune—so unexpected amidst his softness—made her glance at him with shy perplexity. "My—my fortune, sir?"

"It is impossible not to think of it," he said smoothly, "when one sees so gentle a nature bound by circumstance. I would not have you suppose the world values you only for what you possess; but neither should it forget the honour of deserving it."

While these words were passing in the parlour, another conversation of consequence was taking place in the hall. Lady Catherine stood receiving the compliments of several guests, with Mr Darcy at her side. Observing a brief interval, Miss Bingley advanced with proper deference, and said, in a tone of quiet earnestness,

"Your ladyship will forgive me, I hope, for speaking plainly; but I believe Mr Ravenshaw's attentions to Miss de Bourgh this evening are not altogether what they ought to be."

Lady Catherine turned immediately—her manner composed, though her eye expressed a quick intelligence.

Darcy interposed. "I observed something myself— an air of particularity which I did not wholly approve. Pray, Miss Bingley, your reasons?"

"I have known the gentleman's manner too well, madam," replied Caroline. "He once professed himself devoted to me; and, when refused, directed his gallantry elsewhere. I cannot see your daughter so addressed without alarm. His conduct this evening bears the same appearance which once deceived me."

Lady Catherine looked grave, though not incredulous. "You are very right to mention it," said she. "Such candour, from one so well acquainted with the gentleman, merits acknowledgment. I am obliged to you."

The calm assurance of Miss Bingley's tone—so unlike her former vanity—left Darcy in no doubt of her sincerity. He turned to Lady Catherine.

"If you will excuse me, madam," said he, with quiet resolution, "I shall look into the matter at once."

Her ladyship inclined her head with stately approval. "Pray do, nephew; I depend upon your judgement."

Darcy bowed and looked about him; perceiving that Miss de Bourgh was no longer in the hall, he quitted it without delay.

In the parlour, a firm, unhurried step was heard advancing along the passage. Ravenshaw's expression changed; the colour left his face for an instant, and his composure faltered. A moment later Mr Wickham appeared in the doorway.

"I beg your pardon," said he, with a bow towards Anne, "but I fear Miss de Bourgh's fortune is scarcely a fit subject for discussion, sir."

His glance towards Ravenshaw was cool but steady; then, turning to Anne, his manner softened.

"Permit me to conduct you back to your mother, Miss de Bourgh. She grows uneasy at your absence."

Ravenshaw's smile did not reach his eyes.

Anne accepted Wickham's offered arm. "Yes—pray," said she softly. "I would not have her alarmed."

As they quitted the room, they encountered Mr Darcy, whose look conveyed both astonishment and relief.

"You will find Mr Ravenshaw in the parlour," said Wickham quietly. "I shall restore Miss de Bourgh to her ladyship."

Darcy inclined his head in brief approval, and the two passed on. Darcy entered. His countenance was composed, his manner decisive. "Your conduct while a guest at Pemberley, sir," said he, "has been most unbecoming. You will retire to your chamber immediately, and quit this house at first light. I must also entreat that you refrain, in future, from seeking the acquaintance of any member of my family—Miss Bingley not excepted."

Ravenshaw's bow was slow and formal. "Your

wishes, Mr Darcy, shall be observed."

"See that they are, sir."

Wickham led Miss de Bourgh through the adjoining passage into the great hall, where the sound of music and conversation still prevailed. Lady Catherine, who had just concluded a sentence of importance to Colonel Fitzwilliam and Miss Bingley, turned at their approach and started visibly.

"Mr Wickham!" cried she, her astonishment for a moment overpowering ceremony. "You are the last person I expected to see in attendance upon my daughter. Pray, where is my nephew—and why has Anne quitted the ballroom?"

Wickham bowed with respectful composure.

"Your ladyship need not be alarmed. Miss de Bourgh was merely a little overcome by the heat, and Mr Darcy remained behind to attend to a matter requiring his notice. He desired that I should have the honour of restoring your daughter to your care."

Lady Catherine's colour rose; her surprise was not diminished, though her dignity soon reasserted itself.

"Indeed! Then I am obliged to you, Mr Wickham. Anne, you had best sit here a few moments; the air must now be more temperate. Mr Darcy, I trust, will rejoin us directly."

Anne obeyed in silence; her eyes were downcast, but her breathing had grown easier.

Lady Catherine's composure returned as swiftly as it had been shaken. Though she had long been disposed to think ill of Mr Wickham, the propriety of his manner admitted no censure. Her astonishment, once subsided, left only a sense of gratified importance at being so publicly appealed to.

"Very well," said she, with measured condescension. "You have acted with attention, Mr Wickham—quite as a man of sense ought. I am glad to see that good conduct is not beyond hope in every quarter."

Wickham bowed again, accepting the compliment with respectful gravity, and withdrew into the passing crowd. Colonel Fitzwilliam, who had observed the scene, caught his aunt's expression—half perplexity, half pride—and could not forbear a smile. Lady Catherine, perfectly restored to herself, resumed her discourse; and the bustle of the hall went on undisturbed.

When Darcy reappeared, he paused a moment upon the threshold, satisfied that tranquillity was restored. Then, catching sight of Bingley near the door, he crossed to him and spoke in a low tone.

"Ravenshaw has exceeded all propriety," said he. "I have requested that he retire to his chamber, and he is to quit Pemberley at first light."

Bingley looked surprised, yet his countenance expressed nothing but concern. "I am sorry to hear it, Darcy. I know you would not act without cause."

"You do me justice," returned Darcy. "It is unpleasant, but necessary. I shall explain all when there is leisure."

Bingley inclined his head with friendly warmth. "Say no more—you have my full confidence. Only let the evening end as peaceably as it began."

Darcy's smile was slight but grateful. "That is my hope." With this assurance, he moved away, his composure unshaken, and soon perceived Wickham at a little distance.

"A word, sir, if you please." They stepped aside to a quiet corner.

"You are acquainted, I believe, with my estate of Oakmere," began Darcy, "on the border of Staffordshire—some twenty miles distant, and about ten from the turnpike to Ashbourne."

"I remember it well," replied Wickham. "We passed it on our way."

"The manor-house now stands unoccupied," said Darcy. "Its late tenant being deceased, I see no reason it should remain so. I am indebted to you, Wickham, and deeply sensible of the service you have rendered my cousin this evening. If you are disposed to undertake the management of the property, you may reside there while the agency continues in your care. It will yield an income of four hundred a year—sufficient for comfort, if prudently governed. The house is not large, yet perfectly respectable; and should you shew steadiness in the discharge of your trust, I believe it may secure alike your credit and your family's comfort."

Wickham was silent for a moment, his usual ease quite gone. "You are very generous, Darcy," he said at length. "I will not abuse your confidence. You shall have no cause to regret this kindness."

Darcy inclined his head. "Let it then be my Christmas gift to you—and to Mrs Wickham. I am persuaded your reformation is sincere; see that it continues to deserve belief."

Wickham's voice, though low, was steady. "It shall, sir; and I thank you—from my heart."

He went directly to his wife and, bending to Lydia's

ear, told in two sentences what Mr Darcy had done. "Oakmere!—La!" cried she, in a half-whisper that was none. "A house of our own, and four hundred a year!— not so large as Pemberley, to be sure, but I shall make it look prodigiously smart. Mr Darcy is all generosity!" With that she flew to her mother, who, being informed in equal brevity, lifted her hands in rapture and—within five minutes—had made the whole room sensible that Mr Darcy was, in her phrase, "the best of men."

The musicians striking up anew, the ball recovered its brightness; and if a certain gentleman was observed no more that evening, no one who mattered appeared the poorer for his absence.

CHAPTER THE TWELFTH

"When vanity departs, contentment may enter in its place."

In a brief interval between sets, the movement of the company subsided into a cheerful murmur. Georgiana, standing with Kitty and Mary near the lower end of the hall, where the light fell softly from the gallery above, caught sight of Anne seated beside her mother. Her countenance, pale and dispirited, could not be mistaken. The colour which had lately animated her was quite fled; her hands were folded upon her lap, her eyes fixed on the ground, and her whole air expressed a dejection that moved Georgiana exceedingly.

"She looks quite overset," she whispered. "Poor Anne! We cannot leave her so. Will you come with me to persuade her from her mother's side? A little quiet in the music-room may revive her spirits."

Mary and Kitty readily agreed; and together they approached Lady Catherine, who was discoursing with great solemnity to Colonel Fitzwilliam and Miss Bingley.

"If your ladyship will permit," said Georgiana, with gentle firmness, "Anne has been much fatigued, and we would beg her company in the music-room for a few minutes. The air there is cooler, and she might be refreshed by a little quiet."

Lady Catherine looked earnestly at her daughter; and for once her habitual authority yielded to solicitude. "You are very considerate, my dear," said she. "Anne has indeed been a little shaken. It will do her good to be with you and Miss Bennet and Miss Kitty Bennet awhile. Only see that she is not left alone—and that she rests."

Anne rose immediately, grateful yet subdued, and allowed herself to be guided from her mother's side, while Lady Catherine watched them depart with a look more approving than she had ever before bestowed upon a scheme not her own.

Once withdrawn from the crowd, the four young ladies proceeded along the corridor to the familiar music-room, where the lamps burned softly upon the polished instruments and garlands of evergreen. The hum of the ball reached them only as a distant murmur, and the stillness of the room was a relief to every ear.

Mary opened the pianoforte and began a soothing air, her touch gentle and well-governed. Kitty, standing near, joined her in a low sweet voice that seemed rather to soothe than to display; and the soft notes, mingling with the faint hum of the ball, diffused a calm over the little room. Georgiana seated herself beside Anne, speaking only now and then in that low, affectionate tone which wins confidence without effort. Their united kindness had the happiest effect; and by degrees the colour stole back into Anne's cheeks, and the shadow that had clouded her spirits began to lift.

"I am very much obliged to you," said she at last. "It was foolish to feel so overcome—but everything to-night has been so new to me."

"It was not foolish," said Georgiana softly. "The crowd, the noise, the brightness—it might weary anyone unused to it. You have borne it extremely well, and I daresay you will feel easier after a little quiet."

Anne's eyes glistened; she pressed Georgiana's hand and could only whisper, "You are all too good."

While this little circle of kindness was thus engaged, another scene of equal interest passed in the great hall. Mr Hartwell, after much reflection and several half-formed resolutions, at length sought out Mr Bennet, whom he found surveying the company from an arm-chair in a posture of placid observation.

"Mr Bennet," began he, with a composure that ill concealed his earnestness, "I must entreat your indulgence for a question that concerns your daughter—Miss Mary."

Mr Bennet's eye twinkled. "Sir, you could not have chosen a subject more certain of my attention."

"I so admire her good sense, her gentleness, and the steadiness of her principles," Hartwell continued. "If you see no objection, it is my most sincere wish to address her with the hope of obtaining her hand."

Mr Bennet regarded him a moment in silence, half serious, half amused. "You astonish me only by your discernment," said he at last. "Mary has often complained that nobody reads her sermons to advantage; I begin to think you have profited by them better than any man alive. If her inclination accords with yours, you shall have my hearty consent."

Hartwell bowed, deeply gratified. "You do me the greatest honour, sir. I shall speak to her as soon as may be permitted."

"Then God speed you," returned Mr Bennet.

Hartwell thanked him with feeling and withdrew. Mr Bennet, left to his reflections, smiled over the fire at what he termed "the uncommon prevalence of matrimony in one family."

After a moment, he rose, and—rather to Mrs Bennet's astonishment—approached her with an air almost gallant. "My dear," said he, offering his hand, "will you do me the honour of a dance?"

She looked up in unaffected wonder, but made no answer beyond placing her hand in his. When they had taken a few turns, he said, in a tone half playful, half sincere, "Do you remember our first, when we were young?" She coloured, and nodded that she did.

"I fell in love with you then," he continued, with a smile not wholly ironical; "and after all these years, with all our joys and follies, I find myself no wiser—but quite as much in love." Mrs Bennet, overcome by so unexpected a declaration, could only curtsey at the close, declaring that her nerves had never been so agreeably affected.

While Lady Catherine was still discoursing upon the evening's events, Colonel Fitzwilliam, who stood beside her with Miss Bingley on the other side, turned slightly towards the latter and said, with unaffected sincerity, "Miss Bingley, I cannot withhold my thanks for the service you rendered my aunt and cousin this evening. It was a generous act—and one that does you honour."

Caroline's colour rose, though her manner remained composed. "I did only what was proper, Colonel," said she quietly. "I could not bear to see Miss de Bourgh deceived as I once was."

"Proper, perhaps—but by no means common," he returned. "Few would have shewn such courage with so much discretion. I am proud to call you my friend, Miss

Bingley; and, if I may add it, proud to see my aunt indebted to your sense and steadiness."

Her eyes met his then—steadily, yet with a brightness that betrayed her pleasure. "You are very obliging, Colonel Fitzwilliam. I had not thought my conduct worth such notice."

"It is worth much," said he warmly. "And if my esteem may serve as any recompense, you already possess it."

Lady Catherine, who had followed this exchange with evident satisfaction, inclined her head towards Caroline. "My nephew does you no more than justice, Miss Bingley. You have shewn a propriety and good sense quite of the first order. I have long said that discernment is the true mark of breeding, and yours has been most handsomely proved."

Caroline's curtsey was graceful and sincere. "Your ladyship is all kindness. I am happy if my small service has merited your approval."

At that instant the music recommenced. Colonel Fitzwilliam made a motion towards the dancers, and Caroline's countenance shewed ready assent; but before they could take their places, Elizabeth and Jane approached from the farther side of the room.

"Miss Bingley," said Elizabeth gaily, "have you seen our sisters? Kitty and Mary have quite disappeared, and there are two or three gentlemen standing about in great perplexity, as if robbed of their partners."

Colonel Fitzwilliam, whose expression betrayed amusement rather than alarm, said, "They are perfectly safe, I assure you. Miss Darcy led them to the music-room not ten minutes past. Lady Catherine gave permission for Miss de Bourgh to rest there awhile, and the others attend her."

Jane looked relieved. "Then we must go to them, Lizzy. I would not have Mama discover their absence and make a scene of it."

Elizabeth smiled. "A wise precaution indeed. Miss Bingley, will you accompany us?"

Caroline turned to the Colonel with composed regret. "Pray excuse me, Colonel Fitzwilliam; Mrs Darcy has need of me for a moment. I shall hope we may dance later."

"I shall hold you to the promise," said he, bowing with good humour.

With a slight smile, Caroline joined Elizabeth and Jane. The three ladies quitted the hall together. The sound of the orchestra soon faded to a distant murmur, replaced by the quieter air of the house beyond. At the corridor's end the music-room stood open, bright and tranquil; and as they entered, the tender notes of the pianoforte, mingled with a low sweet voice, met their ears.

Caroline went directly to Anne's side, her manner all kindness and concern. "My dear Miss de Bourgh," said she earnestly, taking her hand, "I hope you are better. You must not reproach yourself for what has passed. No woman living could have foreseen such artifice, and no one of sense will think the less of you for having been deceived by it."

Her words astonished the room. Georgiana, Mary, and Kitty looked on in silent wonder, scarcely crediting such tenderness from that quarter.

Anne, moved by the compassion in Caroline's voice,

faltered out a brief account—how Mr Ravenshaw's attentions had seemed at first no more than politeness, how his manner had grown so earnest she scarcely knew how to answer him, and how, in the end, she had felt both flattered and frightened by what she did not fully understand.

Caroline listened gravely. "I know too well how such a man can work upon a woman's feelings," she said at last. "I once believed his professions myself, and the discovery of their insincerity was bitter indeed. Let us resolve, my dear Miss de Bourgh, never to give him power over our thoughts again—but to remember only the lesson."

Anne's eyes filled with tears, but they were tears of gratitude rather than shame. She pressed Caroline's hand. "Indeed I will," she said softly. "And I thank you—for speaking as no one else could have done."

The two ladies exchanged a look of perfect understanding; and from that moment, an unexpected friendship began between them—founded not on vanity, but on sympathy and strength.

The stillness that had followed their reconciliation was gently broken by a burst of lively sound from the doorway. "There you are!" cried Lydia, sweeping into the room in all her brightness. "La! I have looked everywhere for you. What is happening in here—some sort of club? Am I invited?"

Kitty laughed outright, and even Mary smiled. "We were only talking," said she, "though it might pass for a meeting, if you choose to call it so."

"A meeting!" repeated Lydia, seating herself without ceremony. "How solemn that sounds. I am glad to have arrived before you elected a president—Lizzy would never let me preside, I know."

Lydia's exclamation still hung in the air when Georgiana, smiling, said softly, "Perhaps it ought to be a club. We have all endured something—each in her own way—and come through it the stronger. Why should we not resolve to stand by one another henceforth?"

"That is very prettily said, my dear," observed Elizabeth, her eyes bright with affection. "A society of sisters—not by blood, perhaps, but by sympathy and good fortune."

Jane pressed her hand. "A fellowship for every season of life," she added. "When we are parted, we may still remember that we have friends who understand."

Caroline, with a composed but genuine smile, said, "Then we must have a name—something that will remind us where this friendship began. What say you to the Pemberley Circle?"

"The Pemberley Circle!" repeated Kitty with delight. "I like that exceedingly—it sounds quite grand."

Anne looked round the room, her colour softly risen. "Whatever it be called," she said, "I shall never forget this night, nor those who helped me to bear it."

"Then it is settled," cried Lydia gaily. "The Pemberley Circle shall meet whenever we are together!"

"And when distance divides us, let remembrance and good-will keep us together," Mary added.

"An excellent point, Mary," said Elizabeth. "Let us be each other's best champions, and never think ill where we might think kindly."

At that moment Darcy, Bingley, and Wickham came in together, all good-humour and brightness; and Hartwell followed a step behind, pausing at the threshold as the scene within met his view.

Darcy looked round the circle of ladies with mingled surprise and amusement. "Upon my word," said he, "we feared a general desertion. The ball is quite at a stand without you."

Bingley laughed. "Indeed, the gentlemen grow desperate. Jane, Lizzy—your partners are wandering about like souls in search of salvation."

Their playful reproaches were received with cheerful protest. Lydia, clapping her hands, cried, "Our secret is out! We are now The Pemberley Circle—a society of strong sisters who mean to stand by one another for ever. But I suppose even the firmest sisterhood must yield to a country-dance."

"Your generosity does you credit, Mrs Wickham," said her husband, bowing with mock gravity. "Come, my love, let us shew them that married happiness can dance as nimbly as any courtship."

"Most wisely spoken," said Darcy, smiling. "May I have the honour of leading Mrs Darcy back to the hall?"

Elizabeth rose, laughing. "With pleasure, sir— though you have interrupted a very solemn inauguration."

General laughter followed, and the ladies rose, gathering their gloves and fans. As they moved towards the door, Hartwell, who had stood a little apart, addressed Mary in a low, earnest voice.

"Miss Bennet," said he, "may I speak with you for a few moments, before you return to the hall?"

Mary coloured slightly and glanced towards Jane and Elizabeth, as if to draw courage from their smiles. Thus reassured, she turned to meet his gaze with composure. "Yes, Mr Hartwell—if you wish it."

Darcy and Bingley exchanged a knowing smile as they led the rest of the company away; and in another moment the room was quiet again, save for the faint echo of music and the gentle flutter of the candles.

Hartwell advanced a few steps, his manner grave but tender. "Miss Bennet," said he, "I shall not pretend to any eloquence, yet I cannot leave this house without speaking what has overcome my heart. From the first of our acquaintance I have admired your good sense, your composure, and that kindly spirit which seeks improvement rather than display. In a world too fond of glitter, you have shewn me what is truly valuable."

Mary, taken by surprise, could not immediately reply; her colour rose, and her hands trembled slightly upon the back of the chair before her.

He went on more earnestly. "If you can think with any favour of a man whose chief ambition is to deserve your esteem, it would be the happiness of my life to call you my wife. I would hope, in sharing our days, to learn wisdom from your steadiness and content from your principles."

Mary found her voice at last. "You do me great honour, Mr Hartwell. I am not accustomed to admiration," she said, with a faint, tremulous smile, "and scarcely know how to deserve it; yet I believe our minds are alike in wishing to do what is right. If such likeness may promise happiness, I think—it may."

A warmth of quiet joy passed over Hartwell's

features. "Then I am the most fortunate of men."

He took her hand with reverence rather than triumph; and as the distant strains of the country-dance swelled once more from the hall, Mary Bennet knew, for the first time in her life, what it was to be truly chosen—and truly understood.

The ladies re-entered the great hall just as a new set was forming, and their appearance was hailed with instant delight. Captain St John, perceiving Kitty among them, hastened forward with such animation that several gentlemen gave way before him; while Mr Hale, approaching from the opposite side, addressed Miss Darcy with a look of unfeigned pleasure. In another moment, all were engaged, and the floor again filled with light steps and happy faces.

Even Miss de Bourgh, persuaded by a courteous neighbour from Lambton, was prevailed upon to stand up; and though her movements were timid at first, she soon discovered a degree of enjoyment that astonished her mother, who watched from her seat with unwonted satisfaction.

At that moment Colonel Fitzwilliam, catching sight of Caroline near the door, approached with a smile. "If you have not quite forgotten your promise, Miss Bingley, will you do me the honour of the last?"

She accepted with a composure that did not disguise her pleasure, and they took their places among the dancers.

When the set concluded, a fresh murmur ran through the company: Mr Hartwell and Miss Mary Bennet had returned. Their countenances told the story before words were spoken; and as the intelligence spread, congratulations and good-humoured exclamations were heard on every side. Mr Bennet surveyed the scene with complacent good humour; Mrs Bennet glowed with rapture; and even Lady Catherine, though momentarily surprised, was at length prevailed upon to declare the match most suitable.

Thus the evening—and with it, the Christmas at Pemberley—ended in perfect harmony: every heart content, every face bright with hope; and the memory of that night was long cherished by all who had shared its happiness.

EPILOGUE

When it was rehearsed to Bingley all that Mr Ravenshaw had attempted—his presumption towards Miss de Bourgh, and the impropriety of his former attentions to his own sister—he was heartily concerned that such deceit should have entered their circle, and sincerely rejoiced that prompt measures had been taken to prevent its continuance. His good humour, though never blind, was quick to forgive where reformation might be hoped, and he declared himself perfectly satisfied that all had ended as well as prudence and kindness could contrive; and, in the serenity that followed the late disturbance, every heart seemed more at ease than before.

The days that followed were among the happiest Pemberley had ever known. With the snow lingering upon the hills and the frost bright upon every hedge, the house stood at the heart of a cheerful little world of its own. There were frequent expeditions into Lambton, when the younger members of the party— Captain St John, Mr Hale, Mr Hartwell, and their fair companions Kitty, Georgiana, Mary, and even Miss de Bourgh—went down to play with the village children and carry them small gifts from Pemberley: currant buns, sugared almonds, and the occasional ribbon or story-book. The sound of laughter followed them home, and even Lady Catherine condescended to approve, declaring that "benevolence, properly directed, is the truest ornament of rank."

Anne's health, long delicate, improved sensibly with her spirits. She was seen daily in the air, and at last, to the delight of the whole party, ventured upon the ice. "Only a turn or two," she protested, but the glow upon her cheek said more than her words.

Caroline Bingley, whose manner had softened into something very near amiability, was often found beside Colonel Fitzwilliam, who appeared to take uncommon pleasure in her society. Once or twice they rode together round the park; and though nothing passed to provoke conjecture, more than one observer was tempted to hope.

Lady Catherine, whose opinion of Miss Bingley had risen with every proof of her discernment and good sense, spoke of her in terms of decided approbation. "Miss Bingley," said she to her nephews, "has shewn a degree of consideration and propriety which does her the greatest credit. Her conduct towards my daughter has been everything that is attentive and becoming; she knows how to speak with respect, and to be silent with intelligence—a talent most uncommon among young women of the day. I am persuaded she would grace any society to which she was admitted."

Before she quitted Pemberley, her ladyship pronounced herself thoroughly satisfied with her visit. "I will own," said she, in the presence of all assembled, "that my nephew has chosen his mistress well. Mrs Darcy does Mr Darcy great credit; and I have rarely seen a household more perfectly ordered."

Elizabeth, smiling, thanked her; and even Darcy, though he made no speech, looked as though he could not deny his aunt's judgement.

A quieter scene passed when Caroline, meeting Mr Wickham near the fire, ventured to ask, "How is it that you are so changed from the man we once knew?"

He was silent a moment, then said simply, "Have you never done anything you deeply regretted—because of those it hurt?"

She looked down. "Yes."

"Then you understand," said he.

Mary and Mr Hartwell were now much engaged in arranging their spring wedding; and the cheer with which every branch of the family entered into their concerns left no doubt of the general satisfaction.

Thus the Christmas at Pemberley passed into a memory of brightness and affection. And when, after Twelfth Night, the guests dispersed—to Cheshire, to London, and to their several homes—each carried away the sense that no season had ever been spent with more happiness, or left behind a truer spirit of good-will.

And now, a little Christmas offering for our friends

Grace at Barton Cottage

AP MADDOX

A SEASON OF CHEER

The short days before Christmas brought to Barton Cottage a cheerfulness no scanty fortune could repress. Though the season altered nothing in their simple way of living, it lent every task a brighter air. Marianne and Margaret returned from the hedgerows one crisp morning with baskets of holly and ivy—to be set by in the porch until Christmas Eve, when custom allowed them to deck the rooms. The fragrance of rosemary filled the little house.

Their preparations were not without expectation, for the road from Delaford was daily watched. Mr and Mrs Edward Ferrars were near enough for frequent visits; and Elinor's quiet happiness—rational, useful, and serene—seemed to spread itself through the family as naturally as the warmth of a well-tended fire.

Colonel Brandon, too, was often at hand. That his happiness depended in no slight degree upon the peace of a certain young lady was a truth suspected by every member of the family and proclaimed (with a tactlessness that became in him a sort of comic virtue) by Sir John Middleton to the entire neighbourhood. Yet the Colonel's attentions were of a nature to alarm no one, least of all the object of them. He came and went with a deference that approached delicacy; he brought a book, or a small basket of hothouse grapes from Delaford's frames; he took pains—unseen, and therefore the more engaging—to inquire after an elderly cottager's rheumatism, or to repair a paling that the wind had loosened; and then he sat content, if content it could be called, to hear Marianne play without a word that could be taxed with presumption.

Marianne herself had undergone a change not to be mistaken by those who loved her. There was a steadiness in her manner that no longer sprang from the ardours of an hour, but from the recollection of a year. She played, she read, she walked—still with feeling, but with feeling schooled; a sentiment refined by patience, not extinguished by it. The fervour remained—indeed it would ever be part of her character—but it had been chastened into grace.

One morning, when a hoar frost lay white upon the meadow and traced delicate embroidery along the hedges, Colonel Brandon arrived from Delaford, bringing with him Mrs Ferrars, who had accepted his offer of conveyance to Barton Cottage. He had sent to Exeter for some new music, which he hoped might please Marianne. Together they found the little house in a cheerful bustle of ribbon and twine.

"My dear Colonel," cried Mrs Dashwood, "you are come in good time to judge of our intended festoon. Marianne insists that, when we hang it on Christmas Eve, it must droop to the very fender, and I declare we shall be forever pushing it up with the poker."

Marianne laughed. "Mama, the eye requires the graceful line. If the garland is hung too high, it will cut the room short and destroy all proportion."

"That is a crime never to be forgiven," said Elinor, unfastening her pelisse. "We must not be guilty of deforming the proportions of a room that has so few inches to spare."

"Ah! Elinor," said Mrs Dashwood, "you appear and all is set to rights. Colonel Brandon, we shall adopt whichever arrangement Elinor approves, for she has a method that turns even our simplicity into elegance."

The Colonel, with a smile that said enough and not too much, bowed. "If Mrs Ferrars—arranges it, the holly will be perfect in any place, even if it waits a few days for its honour."

"It will be perfect," said Margaret, "when I have found my mislaid paper stars. Colonel, did you see them flying anywhere along the lane?"

"I did not, Miss Margaret," he replied, "but if a troop of stars had been abroad, I am persuaded they must have sought your company again."

Margaret, pleased to be so addressed, ran off in search of her treasures.

Marianne, who till now had been laughing, recollected the small parcel in his hand. "You have brought something for us, Colonel?" said she, with a look of real pleasure.

"A trifle," he replied. "Some music I thought might suit your taste."

Her expression softened. "Then I am doubly obliged—for the thought, and for the confidence. I shall value it."

The simple civility, uttered without affectation, gave the Colonel more happiness than any flourish of gratitude could have done.

Mrs Dashwood turned to Elinor. "You have come without Edward? I had hoped—"

"He is detained at Delaford," said Elinor with her accustomed composure. "A parishioner has fallen ill, and he would not leave the poor man without comfort."

"Then Heaven reward his goodness," cried Mrs Dashwood warmly. "He is an excellent young divine."

"And," added Marianne, "authority is only tolerable when it is the companion of kindness. Edward has both."

"And some men," said Mrs Dashwood, "have kindness without authority."

Marianne would not raise her eyes, yet their colour deepened, as if some inward conviction quickened her.

"You must both dine with us to-day, if you are not otherwise engaged," said Mrs Dashwood. "We expect Sir John to call about the carols and the parcels for Whitwell. He declares he will make a procession of us all, and that we must have a drum; though I have protested against the drum."

"Thank you, Mama," said Elinor with her gentle composure. "I shall be very happy to stay."

"And I," added the Colonel, "shall be honoured to join you."

If his look, as it rested a moment on Marianne, expressed more gratitude than the occasion demanded, it was a warmth so modestly contained that it could offend no one.

A SEASON OF COMPASSION

They had not long to wait for Sir John. He came as he always came—like a gust of cheerful wind that blew the door open wide—and was half-way across the parlour with both hands out before the servant could announce him.

"Happy Christmas!—or as near as may be," he cried. "Well, ladies, well, Brandon! I have brought you news—good, bad, I cannot say; but news it is, and that at least will furnish talk enough for three dinners."

"We are so comfortably supplied with conversation, Sir John," said Elinor, smiling, "that we can spare a little to the poor."

"Spare me none to-day," he returned, lowering his voice as if about to impart a secret and then, with characteristic inconsistency, pronouncing it aloud: "I have brought a guest."

"A guest?" repeated Mrs Dashwood, with that hospitable readiness which had never yet been checked by the size of her rooms. "You know, Sir John, that any friend of yours—".

The figure that followed Sir John through the door checked her speech. He removed his hat; grief and penance had worn their traces upon a countenance once too assured. Mr Willoughby bowed—first to Mrs Dashwood, then to Elinor—and lastly to Marianne, whose complexion had paled in an instant, though her posture did not waver.

Colonel Brandon rose, and his bow, though perfectly

correct, was such as might have been cut from ice.

Sir John nevertheless persisted in good humour. "I told him he must come," said he. "We are none of us saints, and at Christmas especially we must all be forgiven something. Come, Willoughby, we shall have the ladies carolling before the week is out, and you shall turn music-leaf as well as any man."

Mrs Dashwood found her voice. "Mr Willoughby, you are welcome to our fire. Pray be seated."

The ladies, thus invited to composure, resumed their seats also.

He spoke low. "Madam, I am sensible of your goodness—and undeserving of it."

Elinor inclined her head slightly. "Sir," she said, and nothing more.

Marianne clasped the arm of her chair. "Sir," she said after a moment, "I hope you are—well." The final word, poor and inadequate, was uttered with a steadiness that astonished Margaret, and moved Elinor to a silent, grateful admiration.

Willoughby's reply was strangled in his throat and did not come. He sat where Mrs Dashwood indicated; Sir John, with a bustling benevolence, called for spiced wine; and Colonel Brandon resumed his seat with a quiet severity that communicated more than any accusation could.

Sir John, after describing the intended expedition to Whitwell, the arrangements for a small Christmas Eve party at Barton Park, and the near-miraculous excellence of his own cellar that year, came at last—by circuitous, and therefore inevitable degrees—to the subject of his friend's altered circumstances.

"Poor Willoughby!—you all know—No? Well, you shall know. The truth must be told to spare our friend the trouble of it. He has suffered—a heavy loss. Mrs Willoughby—"

"Sir John," Willoughby said, with effort but civility, "I thank you—I will speak for myself."

Mrs Dashwood's hand, long employed upon the fringe of her shawl, now came to rest. Elinor sat very still. Marianne's eyes, which had been fixed upon the tassel of the bell-pull, now lifted to his.

"I am widowed," said Willoughby simply. "My wife—the babe—came too soon, and both were taken home to rest. It is but two months since, and I have nothing left to say that is not a reproach to myself." His mourning, still too new for habit, seemed to sit upon him like a visible weight.

The silence that followed was profound. Mrs Dashwood's first movement was towards compassion—indeed, it was her nature—and she pressed her handkerchief to her eyes. Elinor, though her mind darted at once to all that had passed—her sister's anguish, the explanations so late and so imperfectly made—could not, for the moment, deny the claim of so evident a sorrow. Marianne's expression altered not to agitation but to pity; the sound of a grief that had some truth in it could never be indifferent to her.

Colonel Brandon, who alone among them knew, in its full extent, the measure of Willoughby's offences, was silent; yet the hand that rested upon his knee clenched, as his thoughts turned to the infant committed to his protection—still living, and fatherless.

Sir John cleared his throat. "Well! We shall not be melancholy while we have Christmas before us. We must all be friends. Willoughby shall dine with us at Barton Park; the neighbourhood will show him every civility, and we will have none of these long faces. Mrs Dashwood, you will come, all of you; Brandon, of course; and Edward and Mrs Ferrars too, if they can be prevailed upon—"

"You need not prevail upon us," said Elinor, smiling. "Mr Ferrars has promised to visit his parishioners early, and we shall be free by noon. We would not miss the evening for the world."

"Excellent!" cried Sir John. "Then I shall command the frost to be limited to the hedges."

When Sir John and Willoughby had withdrawn—Sir John declaring he must carry his guest off to secure him from too many tears and too little claret—there was a little bustle in the cottage, and then a quiet fell which obliged someone to speak.

Mrs Dashwood spoke first. "My dears," she began, struggling between prudence and pity, "whatever may be said of Mr Willoughby—and much is to be said against him—I cannot think of his loss without pain."

"No one could, Mama," said Elinor gently. "Compassion is always in season. Only let us not mistake compassion for confidence."

Marianne walked to the window, touched the frosted pane, and returned. "He is altered," she said at last. "It would be senseless to deny it. Suffering has enlarged him—or at least humbled him."

Elinor's look—tender, steady, and a little anxious— rested on her sister. "Humility may be a good beginning," she said, "but it is not the whole of reformation."

Mrs Dashwood glanced at Colonel Brandon, who had remained, though with the modesty of a man ready to vanish at the least sign of being in the way. "Colonel," she said, "what say you?"

"That Mrs Ferrars speaks for us all," he replied. "Compassion must be exercised; confidence must be earned."

Marianne's voice was warm; there was no mistaking its sincerity, nor the gratitude in her look. "I thank you, Colonel, for choosing so equitable an answer."

He bowed. "Miss Marianne does me too much honour."

When Elinor and her mother retired a few minutes later to see to the arrangement of the dinner, Margaret flew upstairs in pursuit of her missing paper stars, protesting that, if they were truly lost, she must make new ones before nightfall; and thus Marianne and the Colonel were left for a few moments together.

"You do not think me hard," she said at last, with her frankness, "if I admit pity without—without the wish to feel more?"

"I think you just," he said.

"And you—" She hesitated, and then, as if choosing courage—"You have felt pity where others—where I— was unjust."

"Miss Marianne," he answered, his tone low, "I have felt everything that could be felt—pity, anger, fear— fear most of all when your life was endangered; and afterwards—gratitude."

She could not meet his eyes; she looked instead at the fire, where the coals burned steadily, without show. "I am learning, Colonel," she said softly, "to value what endures."

He did not trust himself to reply. It was enough that she had said it.

A SEASON OF CHARITY

By Sir John's decree, the next day had been devoted to the carols and parcels for Whitwell. A small procession, cheerful as a Christmas ribbon and scarcely more formidable, set out from Barton Park—Lady Middleton wrapped in furs; Mrs Jennings with a basket of mince pies; Sir John with a lantern that he swung though the sun was high in the sky; and Margaret and the Middleton children wrapped more in laughter than in cloaks.

Elinor, Edward, and Colonel Brandon, having come that morning from Delaford, joined the party at the gate of the park. Even Mr Willoughby was there, persuaded by Sir John that a little good-will could do no harm at Christmas. His countenance was grave, yet there was a softness in his manner which spoke of humility rather than pride.

The villagers, in anticipation of the merriment, were already gathered in the little square before the church—a place hemmed round with cottages and brightened now by evergreens and the gleam of red cloaks and shawls. Sir John bustled among them, calling out names, directing the children into lines, and proclaiming that no throat should go uncarolled and no hand unfilled. Mrs Jennings dispensed her mince pies with the air of one bestowing jewels; Lady Middleton approved whatever her husband declared delightful.

Willoughby took charge of the parcels for the children, stooping to hand each small bundle with a few kind words. When a little girl curtsied and pressed a sugared cake to her lips in thanks, he turned aside for a moment, his composure shaken, and brushed his hand quickly across his eyes. Marianne, seeing it, felt neither confusion nor pain—only that solemn compassion which comes of understanding rather than illusion.

Then the carols began. Marianne sang. Her voice, though somewhat less brilliant than formerly—perhaps because she no longer flung it upon the listener, but gave it rather—had gained a tenderness that penetrated. She sang of tidings of comfort and joy, and though she had no vanity in the display, more than one villager looked at her with the gratitude accorded to a benefactor rather than to a singer. The Colonel stood a little apart, his hat in his hands, and it seemed to Marianne that the song was not wholly hers while she performed it; part of it belonged to him, who had waited through its first notes before he could hear the rest.

A SEASON OF PEACE

The frost lay thick upon the fields and sparkled on every branch as the morning of Christmas Eve dawned upon Barton Cottage, which, till now, had only promised its Christmas cheer, was all alive with preparation. The holly and ivy were brought in; ribbons were adjusted, candles trimmed, and Margaret, having at last recovered her mislaid paper stars, was busily affixing them wherever she could find a vacant beam or windowpane.

Marianne moved more softly than usual, but with an expression of content that needed no explanation; and Mrs Dashwood, whose heart was always fullest when her hands were busy, could hardly decide whether the house looked more cheerful or her daughters happier.

By afternoon, their labours were completed, and the time had come to dress for Sir John's much-anticipated Christmas Eve party at Barton Park.

Sir John's party was as unavoidable as winter. Barton Park, with its cheerful rooms and absence of any ceremony that could be mistaken for restraint, was the kind of theatre in which every private feeling finds public observation. Mrs Jennings, happy and inquisitive as ever, had joined the Middletons, armed with conjectures which she applied liberally to every look and movement of every creature in the room.

"Well!—here we are again," she cried to Elinor, who arrived on Edward's arm, "and I declare I am so glad to see you as Mrs Ferrars, that I shall never call you Miss

Dashwood again—no, not if I live to be a hundred. How well you look, to be sure. And Mr Ferrars, how do you do, sir?—and how is your mother?—though, la! I do not ask after people I never see."

"Then you must reserve your kindness for those you do see," said Elinor, smiling.

"I shall, my dear; you may depend upon it. And where is your sister?—Ah! there she is. How handsome she grows! And so composed!—there is not half the flutter I used to see. Well, I do like to see a girl profit by experience. And the Colonel too!—You cannot run away from me, Colonel, so do not try. I shall have a peep at your face, and if I see you frowning at Miss Marianne, I shall shake my head at you."

"Then I must not frown," said the Colonel, with such gentleness that Mrs Jennings was delighted and declared him the most sensible man alive.

"Ah, well!" cried she, "we must all be sensible now and then, mustn't we?—especially at Christmas, when even the worst of us deserve a little good-will. Poor Mr Willoughby!—I cannot help being sorry for the creature, though I would not have him within twenty miles of Miss Marianne again for the world. Still, to lose his wife and child so suddenly—it is a sad business indeed! I always said he had more heart than head, and see how dearly he has paid for it."

Elinor coloured slightly, while the Colonel, with a composure that did him credit, replied only, "Your compassion, ma'am, does you honour."

It was impossible to be long at Barton Park without encountering Mr Willoughby. He entered, grave, subdued, and in a plain black coat that argued neither poverty nor vanity. He bowed to Mrs Dashwood with a respect that no effrontery could counterfeit; to Elinor with a demeanour which asked nothing and thanked her for less; and to Marianne with a look which, though instantly suppressed, betrayed the tenderness he could not conquer.

"Mr Willoughby," said Sir John, calling him from across the room, "you shall stand here and help me judge the dancing. Connoisseurs must be employed in their art."

"I have no title to the office," he answered quietly, "but I will stand where you please."

Music began. The younger folks danced; the older looked on and recollected; Mrs Jennings directed everybody's steps with great satisfaction to herself and great confusion to the figures. Marianne declined dancing at first; Elinor, understanding her, sat by her side with perfect cheerfulness, making no effort to urge what she would not have urged in herself.

Presently, Sir John, who could not endure to see two ladies unemployed, arrived to carry Elinor off to a country-dance; Edward, with an air of consenting to be happy, received her; and Marianne, thus left, found Colonel Brandon standing near, not close enough to claim her hand, not distant enough to appear indifferent.

"If you will not dance," he said, "may I stand here in idleness beside you?"

"Idleness," said Marianne, with a look half playful, "is the occupation you least deserve."

"Then I shall call it felicity."

She looked away, smiling. The moment, delicate and

not to be enlarged without inaccuracy, was interrupted by Willoughby, who, having conquered the scruples that had restrained him, now approached.

"Miss Dashwood," he said, "might I engage your attention for a few moments where it is quieter?"

Marianne rose. "Colonel," said she, "I will return to my seat presently."

Brandon bowed and withdrew, as a man retires from a room in which he has left his heart.

Willoughby led her to the great bow-window where the garden, white and faintly shining beneath the moon, lay still as a drawing. He paused, as if the silence itself must be acknowledged, and then began.

"I shall not merit forgiveness by speaking of my sufferings," said he. "I have no claim on your pity. Yet I must say—if only once—that I have never ceased to love you."

Marianne did not answer. He continued, hurriedly, as if words alone could keep despair at bay.

"I have been carried, like a reed, by every current that promised ease or elevation. I betrayed myself; I betrayed you—Heaven knows I abhor the recollection. If I could purchase your good opinion by any sacrifice—short of honour, for I have learned at last what that means—I would make it gladly. Miss Dashwood—Marianne—if I may call you so once more?"

"You may call me nothing but Miss Dashwood," she said—without asperity, but without hesitation.

He bowed his head. "Then let me at least say this: I am not the same man."

Marianne's voice was calm. "No," she said, "you are

not. Sorrow has changed you. And I—experience has changed me. You ask for what no longer exists. The girl who believed you infallible—she is not here to answer you."

"Miss Dashwood," he whispered, "if there were a means to begin again—"

"There is no means," she said quietly. "There is only the future; and in that future, I desire serenity."

"And is serenity to be found—" His voice failed; he recovered it. "Is it to be found without love?"

"Without a certain kind of love," she answered, "it is not to be found at all. But love must be joined to esteem, or it is no companion for a lifetime. It must tell as much in silence as in speech; it must be patient to wait as well as quick to feel."

He looked upon her with a desolation that might have moved a sterner heart. "I deserve to lose you," he said. "But I cannot help asking—Is there another who will be more fortunate?"

Marianne's voice was steady. "You have no right to ask me that."

"I have none." He bowed his head. "Forgive me. You owe me nothing. Pray—be happy."

She inclined her head in return. "I wish you peace."

When she rejoined Elinor, who had resumed her seat, the music had begun another set. Elinor looked quietly into her face and read there an answer to many fears.

"You are tired," she said.

"I am—relieved," said Marianne.

Colonel Brandon did not resume his post beside her; prudence, or perhaps delicacy, forbade it. But as he took his leave that night, his eyes met hers for one moment of full understanding, and she felt—not triumph—but rest.

A SEASON OF FAITH

A small stone church stood among yews and gravestones, its bell calling the parish from the frosted fields. The Dashwoods, the Middletons, and Mrs Jennings joined the rest of the congregation on Christmas morning. The service was cheerful; and, as the Dashwoods stood in the porch afterward, Sir John and Mrs Jennings spoke in high spirits of how word had already reached them—by the post-boy—that Colonel Brandon had been abroad in his own parish at first light, distributing small gifts among the children: cakes, apples, and nuts, as was his yearly custom.

Mrs Jennings, with particular satisfaction, declared that she had received further report—by way of the maids—that the Colonel had not forgotten his ward, who, with her child, was comfortably settled in a small cottage in Devonshire, and had likewise received a Christmas-morning visit.

"Though the child came into the world under the worst circumstances," said Mrs Jennings, "she thrives famously; the mother is attentive, and much restored since her confinement. Brandon sees to them both with constant kindness—they want for nothing."

Mrs Dashwood's eyes filled at the account. "I am heartily glad to hear it," said she. "There is no office more sacred than the protection of the helpless; and no man, I am persuaded, fulfils it with greater tenderness and discretion than Colonel Brandon. Pray Heaven the little one may live to bless him for it."

Marianne said earnestly, "It is the truest charity to remember those whom the world is most ready to forget. I honour him the more because he contrives to do good without any parade of it. Such constancy deserves all our esteem."

Later that morning, Colonel Brandon—together with Edward and Elinor, who had come from the Christmas service at Delaford—rode to Barton; and, finding the Dashwoods just returned from their own church, joined them at the gate. When Sir John's account of his morning's benevolence was repeated, the Colonel's modest embarrassment betrayed itself in the quietness of his manner.

The little party proceeded, the air bright with frost and the road glittering beneath the sun. When the carriages drew up at the cottage, Edward alighted, bearing under his arm a parcel of new books for Margaret and a small collection of sermons for Mrs Dashwood, which, he assured her with a twinkle, were less soporific than their titles threatened. Elinor brought patterns for a gown which, properly managed, might enable even Barton's village seamstress to make elegance out of economy—a kindness Marianne received with quiet pleasure rather than girlish delight.

Mrs Dashwood's plum pudding, long anticipated, justified every expectation; and the parlour at Barton Cottage, bright with evergreens and laughter, filled up with that sweet, busy noise which never overpowers and never tires.

After dinner there was music. Marianne played, but not always alone in spirit. Colonel Brandon, who had brought her a new piece from Exeter, stood near the instrument and turned the pages with a care that seemed to know her every movement. Her playing was less impassioned than formerly, yet every note was clear and full of feeling; and when she looked up only once to meet his eyes, the expression that passed between them was as eloquent as any duet. Elinor thought—though she would not have said it—that the accord predicted another harmony not far off.

Later, as dusk drew on and the candles were kindled, Edward was prevailed upon to read aloud the history of the Nativity from the Scriptures; and as the words of faith filled the little parlour, a hush seemed to fall upon them—a peace that was not only domestic, but devout. Afterwards they sang, very softly, *The First Nowell.*

When the reading was ended, the company lingered a little by the fire, unwilling to break the calm that had settled upon them. At length Colonel Brandon rose, and with a warmth that required few words, took his leave—promising to return on the morrow. The hour being late, Edward and Elinor were easily persuaded to remain at the cottage; and when the house grew still at last, its peace seemed the natural close of a day sanctified by affection and by faith.

A SEASON OF MERCY

The air was softened by a faint thaw that made the hedges glitter like glass the following morning. The household at Barton Cottage had passed a tranquil night. Mr and Mrs Ferrars, who had remained after the family party, joined them at breakfast; the talk was cheerful, yet subdued with that quiet satisfaction which follows a day of content.

While they were still at table, a letter was brought in for Mrs Dashwood; and before she could read it, the sound of hoofbeats was heard approaching. A moment later Colonel Brandon was announced. He had come, he said, to inquire after their health and to bring a parcel of gingerbread which Mrs Jennings had declared indispensable to the season.

Mrs Dashwood thanked him for his kindness, then, recollecting the letter, broke the seal and read it. Her countenance changed; after a brief silence she placed it in Elinor's hand with a look of mingled perplexity and compassion. Elinor read, and raised her eyes to her mother and sister with a solicitude she did not attempt to hide.

Edward, who had been watching the scene in thoughtful silence, leaned forward. "I hope there is no ill news," he said kindly.

"It is from Mr Willoughby," said Mrs Dashwood.

Marianne's countenance did not change; she had expected as much, and the subject, though grave, no longer shook her. "To ask for an interview?"

"To request that we will accept his apology—his explanation, he calls it—and to say farewell. He means to leave the county within the week."

Elinor considered. "Mama, will you receive him here?"

"I do not know what is right," said Mrs Dashwood. "My heart is always pleading for the wounded; but I cannot, must not, hazard Marianne's peace."

Marianne spoke with more composure than surprise. "If there is to be an interview, let it be in your presence, Mama—and in Elinor's. I would not wish to deny him a civility that might purchase him a night's rest. But there must be no walks, no music—no past disguised as future."

Colonel Brandon, who had withdrawn to the window, stood looking out upon the pale fields as if the thin frost might instruct him. When Marianne ceased speaking, he turned. "Mrs Dashwood," said he, "if my presence would be any restraint upon you—if it should disturb—pray command me away. But if—if my being within call can be of any comfort—"

Mrs Dashwood, with an impulse she would not have been able to explain even to herself, held out her hand. "You are our friend," she said. "Stay."

He bowed; and as they withdrew to the parlour to receive Mr Willoughby, Colonel Brandon quietly retired to the adjoining room. When Willoughby was announced a few minutes later, the knowledge that the Colonel was near served to strengthen the composure of all who remained.

Willoughby entered with a composure that had in it nothing of indifference. He addressed himself first to

174

Mrs Dashwood, then to Elinor, and lastly to Marianne. Edward, who had risen on his entrance, resumed his seat in silence, while Margaret, wide-eyed and motionless by the hearth, seemed scarcely to breathe. "I am come to say two words," said he: "forgive me—and farewell."

Mrs Dashwood, tremulous, sat. Elinor stood at the corner of the mantel, resolved to speak only when necessity required, and Marianne, who had chosen her seat by the window, where the pale day could look into her face, folded her hands upon her lap.

Willoughby began, and though the substance of his statement was not new—passion had overborne judgment; convenience had seduced honour; pride had delayed apology—there was in his manner a humility that could not be wholly feigned.

"I do not ask," he said in conclusion, "to be thought worthy. I am not. But if it is in your power to believe that suffering has awakened conscience, and that conscience will in time produce character, then I implore you to believe so of me."

Mrs Dashwood wept softly. Elinor, after a moment, said with a firmness that was kind, "Mr Willoughby, we do not doubt that you are in earnest. We wish you no ill—indeed we wish you well."

Edward, who had been silent till now, spoke with quiet gravity. "Mercy," said he, "rejoiceth against judgment; and it is never wasted where repentance has begun. Heaven forgives far more than we deserve; it asks only that we learn to forgive a little in return."

Willoughby bowed his head. "Then I will hope," he said, "to be taught by that mercy."

He turned then to Marianne. "Miss Dashwood, I will not solicit your pardon as if I could claim it; but I entreat your permission to live deserving of it."

Marianne's voice was steady, though her expression softened. "I do forgive you," she said quietly, "with all my heart—and I wish only for peace where pain once was. May that peace find us both."

He was silent for a moment; then, as if recalling something that touched him strangely, he said, "There is a volume of Cowper I once had the insolence to claim here by right of inclination. It is yours; I should be glad to return it."

"It is not mine," said Marianne quietly. "It belongs to the past. Keep it."

He pressed his lips together. "Then I shall give it to someone who will read it better than I did—for instruction, not for vanity." He bowed to Mrs Dashwood and Elinor and looked once at Marianne— a look without demand, and therefore endurable—and was gone.

When the door had closed, the three women remained as they were for several minutes; it was Mrs Dashwood who first rose and went to her daughters. "My love," said she to Marianne, taking her hands, "is your heart at peace?"

"It is," Marianne replied, and the tears that stood in her eyes were not bitter ones.

Elinor stepped softly to the inner door and opened it. The Colonel was there, not listening but waiting, and the look he bent upon them asked a thousand questions and answered them in the same breath.

"Come in, Colonel," said Elinor, with a smile that

trembled.

He entered and, seeing Marianne's calm countenance, drew a long breath he had not permitted himself before. For a moment he hesitated, as though doubtful of intruding upon her composure; then, mastering his diffidence, he crossed the room and stopped beside her chair. His manner was gentle— grave, yet suffused with a warmth that seemed to make the little parlour itself more cheerful.

"Miss Marianne," said he at last, his voice low and steady, "I shall not present myself at Barton Cottage for a day or two; a small matter requires my attention. It is—of a nature that ought not to be delayed."

She nodded, then spoke with a frankness which had become not reckless but brave. "Colonel—"

He looked up.

"I desired to tell you," she said, "that I am—very grateful. Not for today only. For patience."

He could not answer readily, but when he did, it was with a simplicity that dignified feeling. "If there is gratitude," he said, "it is mine."

She smiled, and though he did not approach, the space between them no longer appeared a division but a promise.

Colonel Brandon took his leave and Marianne drew Elinor a little aside, before Edward could convey her back to Delaford.

"Elinor," said Marianne, without preface—for her candour had not forsaken her, though experience had refined it—"I would ask something of you."

"Anything that is mine to give."

"If—if Colonel Brandon should—if he should one

day—" She stopped, not from confusion but from a well-governed emotion that humbled and exalted her together. "If he should say what I believe he may, and what—" She smiled. "What I think I shall be very happy to hear—will you rejoice with me?"

"My dearest Marianne," said Elinor, her eyes shone with more than sisterly pride, "I shall rejoice with all my heart."

Marianne wrapped her arms around Elinor's waist and lay her head upon her shoulder. Elinor, feeling upon her cheek a tear that was not the offspring of pain, thanked Heaven quietly that constancy and kindness were at last to have their reward.

A SEASON OF GRACE

Colonel Brandon had reason to make haste, for Sir John reported that Mr Willoughby intended to quit the neighbourhood within a few days. He therefore dispatched a brief note to Barton Park, requesting, on a matter of urgency, the favour of Mr Willoughby's attendance at Delaford.

Willoughby obeyed, though not without apprehension. That the Colonel should desire an interview with him could promise, he thought, nothing agreeable; and when he was admitted to the library at Delaford, where a low fire glowed, and the Colonel stood by it, grave yet calm, his countenance betrayed no small degree of uneasiness.

Colonel Brandon received him with a consideration the other had never yet experienced from him. "Pray be seated, Mr Willoughby," said he, with uncommon kindness. "You must wonder at my summons."

"I confess I am at a loss," returned Willoughby.

"You are acquainted," resumed the Colonel, after a moment, "with a young woman by the name of Eliza Williams?"

A slight change passed over Willoughby's face. "I am," he answered, in a voice that strove for firmness but did not quite command it.

Colonel Brandon regarded him steadily and spoke with a gravity softened by compassion. "You have sustained a heavy bereavement. Your spirit, I do not doubt, is humbled; and solitude presses the more

179

severely upon a mind that has known a different kind of society. There is, perhaps, a vacancy—an emptiness—which grief alone cannot fill."

At this, Willoughby inclined his head, grateful to be understood where he least expected compassion.

"Yet there is one remembrance," continued the Colonel, more gently still, "which ought not to be lost amidst your sorrows." He paused, as if to allow the recollection to rise, then added, "You have a living child."

Willoughby started; tears rose unbidden to his eyes. In the tumult of recent suffering, that sacred claim had stood too much in shadow; he could only look up, his silence an acknowledgment both of guilt and of feeling.

"There is a little girl—your daughter," said Brandon, "an infant whose life began under disadvantages not of her own making. Her mother, likewise, is in need—not of money only, though that must not be withheld—but of steadiness of character, of that support which gives courage to duty."

Willoughby's expression, compounded of remorse and a dawning, tremulous hope, spoke more than any protestation. He seemed at once ashamed and astonished to be permitted to remember with tenderness.

They need you, Mr Willoughby," said Colonel Brandon; and then, with a warmth he had never before allowed himself, "John, they need you."

The novelty of that address overcame Willoughby; he could not command a word.

Colonel Brandon rose. "If you are equal to the office—if affliction has taught you self-government,

180

and repentance the claims of honour—you will not refuse what is now due."

Willoughby drew a hand across his eyes, wiping tears, and bowed his assent.

"Come, then," said the Colonel. He opened a door from the library into a small inner parlour, where Eliza sat with the child, gently rocking the little creature in her sleep. At their entrance, she looked up; Willoughby's gaze, fixed in wonder and compunction, fell upon the mother and then upon the infant.

"Her name is Grace," said Eliza softly.

Willoughby's answer was only a broken "God bless her"—but it was enough.

Thus it may be said that Colonel Brandon—who, more than any man, might have been justified in sustaining an unalterable resentment towards Mr Willoughby for the injury done to one who had been to him almost a daughter—yet found, in the claims of an innocent infant, motives both to forgive and to hope. For there are few instruments of Providence more powerful in reconciling wounded spirits than a child: their very helplessness pleads for us; they come as a pledge from Heaven, softening severe judgments and binding up hearts that have been cruelly divided.

A SEASON OF HOPE

Colonel Brandon had another reason to make haste. Sir John had long rallied him to be patient—good-humouredly declaring that perseverance must in time be rewarded—but the season for patience had passed. There are hours when hope, long exercised in silence, ripens at last into quiet courage; and such an hour had come for him.

Having seen Willoughby introduced to his daughter, and the hope rekindled in Eliza's eyes that her child might yet know her father, Brandon felt a long tension ease within him. The past had been faced; its duties fulfilled. What remained to him now was the future—and Marianne.

At length Willoughby took his leave, with the promise of returning on the morrow. When all was concluded, Brandon saw Eliza and her child safely conveyed back to their cottage; and then, calling for his horse, he set out through the clear, cold afternoon towards Barton Cottage—every mile seeming shorter than the one before.

He found the family gathered about the parlour fire: Mrs Dashwood at her work, Elinor and Edward in cheerful talk, Margaret carefully taking down her paper stars to lay them by for another Christmas, and Marianne seated at the pianoforte, turning over the new music with a look of tranquil pleasure.

Mrs Dashwood rose to greet him with her

183

accustomed warmth. "My dear Colonel," she cried, "we had not looked for you so soon again, though you are always welcome. You have been abroad in the cold, I see—pray, come to the fire."

"Thank you, ma'am," he replied, drawing nearer, "the air was keen—but the ride was shorter than I could have wished."

Elinor, perceiving in his countenance a resolution too calm to be uncertain, contrived, with her usual delicacy, to remove all interruption. She persuaded Edward to examine with her a passage in the new volume of sermons; Margaret was enlisted to secure her stars in their box; and Mrs Dashwood, smiling through sudden comprehension, resumed her seat. Thus, by gentle degrees, the company disposed itself elsewhere—and Marianne was left, without contrivance yet not by accident, unclaimed.

When the moment came, the Colonel advanced. "Miss Marianne," said he, his voice low but steady, "you once spoke of learning to value what endures. I have sought, in my own imperfect way, to do the same—and in that lesson, I have found no constancy equal to what I feel for you. If your peace can include me—if you could consent to let me guard it rather than disturb it—will you be my wife?"

Marianne looked up, startled only by the tenderness that trembled in his tone. "You have waited," she said softly, "with more constancy than I deserved. If there is happiness to be shared between us, I shall count it my greatest blessing."

He took her hand as one receiving a sacred trust, hope and wonder softening every feature of his countenance. Mrs Dashwood, unable to contain her tears, declared it the sweetest Christmas gift Heaven had ever granted to her family.

Elinor came forward and embraced her sister with affectionate triumph; Edward grasped the Colonel's hand in hearty congratulation; and Margaret, clapping hers together, cried that nothing could ever look so beautiful again as Barton Cottage that night.

The little parlour, bright with evergreens and firelight, seemed to hold within its narrow walls every form of peace that affection, faith, and gratitude could bestow—and thus the season of hope fulfilled its promise.

Reader's Reflections for *A Christmas Beginning – The Pemberley Circle Series – Book 1*

Restoration and Grace

1. *Restoring the Fallen:*
   The story restores those once disgraced (*Wickham*), overlooked (*Mary*), or vain (*Caroline*).
   How does it reconcile charity—civility, kindness, and forgiveness—with the realities of broken hearts and disappointed hopes?
   How does goodness refine society more effectively than resentment or pride?

2. *Three Arcs of Renewal:*
   The novella's three chief threads—Mary and Hartwell's quiet romance, Ravenshaw's deceit (resulting in Caroline's self-reflection), and Wickham's reformation—each portray a kind of redemption.
   Which arc spoke most powerfully to you, and why?
   Which character's transformation resonated most with you?
   In their place, what might you have done differently—or perhaps the same?

Mary Bennet's Transformation

3. *The Education of the Heart:*
   In what subtle ways does Mary's change—from moral rigidity to sincere humility—unfold through her music, her charity, and her eventual acceptance of Mr Hartwell?
   What does their union suggest about quiet virtue finding its due reward?

4. *Confidence and Humility:*
   How might confidence and humility grow together rather than stand opposed?
   Which moments in Mary's story bring these two qualities into harmony?

Caroline Bingley and the Measure of Character

5. *Contrasts of Character:*
   How does the contrast between the characters of Mr Ravenshaw and Colonel Fitzwilliam shape Caroline's awakening?
6. In what ways does this difference teach her to discern true worth from mere polish or charm?
7. *Caroline's Reformation:*
   Caroline's courage in exposing Ravenshaw's deceit marks a change from her earlier vanity.
   How does her friendship with Colonel Fitzwilliam teach her that dignity depends more upon character than affluence?

Anne de Bourgh and the Power of Gentleness

7. *Anne's Awakening:*
   How does Anne's gentle progress—from submission to self-possession—contribute to the story's emotional resolution?
   What role does Georgiana's quiet mentorship play in fostering her growth?
8. *Honour and Independence:*
   How did Anne learn that she could assert independence without wounding her mother's pride?
   What virtue lies in honouring one's parents while still learning to become one's own person?

Mercy, Parenthood, and Redemption

9. *The Reformation of Mr Wickham:*
   What influence might the prospect of fatherhood have had upon Mr Wickham's change of heart?
   How does the responsibility of nurturing another life awaken repentance and resolve?
   (You might reflect on how parenthood—literal or figurative—has matured or softened your own outlook.)
10. *Mercy and Grace:*
    How does Darcy's offer of Oakmere to Wickham embody both mercy and grace?

In what ways does it echo Mr Hartwell's Christmas message:

"Peace does not descend because the world is still, but because forgiveness is alive within it."

The Circle Completed

11. *The Pemberley Circle:*

    When the ladies form "The Pemberley Circle," what does the name signify beyond friendship?

    How does this fellowship heal former rivalries and soften past wounds?

    What might Austen herself have thought of such reconciliation among her heroines?

12. *The Darcys as Moral Anchors:*

    How do Elizabeth and Darcy guide their household without dominating it?

    In what ways do Elizabeth's composure and competence, joined with Darcy's steadiness and judgement, create harmony among so many varied guests?

    What principles of leadership are demonstrated by Darcy and Elizabeth individually and in partnership?

May these reflections invite you to linger at Pemberley a little longer—and, like its circle of friends, to leave with both heart and spirit enlarged.

Reader's Reflections for *Grace at Barton Cottage*
Home and Contentment
1. *The Dashwoods' Christmas at Barton Cottage*
   The simplicity of Barton Cottage, set against the season's cheer, gives the story its warmth.
   How do the Dashwoods' modest circumstances deepen the meaning of generosity, gratitude, and contentment?
   In what ways does the humbleness of their home magnify the richness of their hearts?

Mercy and Peace
2. *Compassion, Mercy, and Peace*
   Compassion and forgiveness move quietly through the tale—from Edward's reflections on mercy to Marianne's gentle restraint.
   How does compassion guide the actions of each character?
   How does mercy, whether received or extended, become the truest instrument of peace?

Love Refined by Time
3. *The Quiet Transformation of Marianne*
   How has Marianne's understanding of love changed since the events of *Sense and Sensibility*?
   In what ways does her calmer nature reveal not the loss of passion, but its maturing into something steadier and more enduring?
4. *Courage and Temptation*
   With scarcely a year passed since her heartbreak, Marianne might easily have yielded again to the memory of Willoughby's affection.
   What gave her the courage to meet him with compassion but not weakness?
   How does her self-command mark the truest proof of her growth?

Sorrow and Redemption

5. *Willoughby's Sorrow and Humbling*
   Once unrepentant, Willoughby becomes a man softened by grief.
   How might the loss of both wife and child have worked more powerfully upon his heart than any reproach could?

Fatherhood and Faith

6. *The Worth of a Father's Presence*
   Colonel Brandon's decision to invite Willoughby into his daughter Grace's life is an extraordinary act of grace.
   What does this reveal about his belief in the importance of a father's role?
   How might the duty of providing for and guiding a child have the power to reform a man's character?

7. *The Patience of Colonel Brandon*
   Brandon's constancy is marked not by pursuit but by forbearance.
   How does his quiet devotion stand in contrast to Willoughby's impetuous love?
   What does his patience teach about steadfast affection and true constancy?

Faith and Renewal

8. *The Season of Hope*
   The tale concludes with a Christmas proposal and the renewal of many hearts.
   What does this "season of hope" suggest about the enduring truth that happiness is not the reward of ease, but the fruit of endurance, faith, and forgiveness?

May these reflections lead you, as they did the Dashwoods, from trial to peace—and from hope deferred to hope fulfilled.

Angel of the Holy Night

AP Maddox

Samuel Hepworth

www.ingramcontent.com/pod-product-compliance
Lightning Source LLC
Chambersburg PA
CBHW050331110726
47899CB00007B/2463